B. D. Pedersen

ALEXANDER 6

Edited by

June Pedersen

4

Preface

My name is Alexander 6. I have been in the military for a number of years and have always been supremely confident in my abilities and those of my fellow troops. As with any military unit you come to consider yourselves the best outfit around and unbeatable. That's the way it should and must be, otherwise you would never survive.

This would prove true in the not-too-distant future when my command was sent out to confront an intrusion into the territory of the Starfield United System. It was felt we had no choice and must take some form of action against the invading forces. What we didn't know was, due to an unforeseen event while in transit, those invaders had already been taken care of. By that I mean they were no longer a military presence that was a threat to the Starfield United System. What we didn't know was we were next. We would be facing forces of the unknown that was beyond anyone's ability to understand or deal with.

They came out of the ground and underbrush around us and tore into my command with such ferocity one could not even begin to grasp what was happening. It was a nightmare, a downright, mind blowing nightmare.

I couldn't blame them for running, I did myself. I ran as if hell itself was right behind me, and the truth is, it was. Nothing could stop them they just kept coming and seemed to have no end to their numbers. Yeah, I ran and I didn't stop until I was out of those wooded areas and up on the side of a mountain.

There I was, in a small cave, cowering as far back in that cave as I could crawl. I just knew something was out there right behind me and coming for me. I have never been as scared as I was at that time. I was so scared my mind had stopped working. All it told me to do was run and then run some more.

It would take me until the next day to calm down and regain my sense of control. I would find myself alone and separated from my command, if I had a command left that is. I was finally able to gain control of myself and started to deal with the results of the attack from the day before.

It was a setting for a whole new life and adventure for me and those of us who survived the attack. What we still had to deal with was the issues of survival in this alien world we had found ourselves in. It was not the world we had been going to in the first place. Well wait a minute, it was but now it was different. It was the right world but it was the wrong world. Know what I mean.

I mean nowhere in the universe had there been a world like this and I've been to a lot of places in this galaxy and still have never seen anything like it. It's crazy as hell and not getting any better. No this was not the world we had set out to defend. No, something had happened from the time we left our Starfield United System base till we arrived here at this world, something strange and forbidding.

In short order we would figure it out and in doing that find ourselves in the fight of our lives in order to survive. It would change our whole attitude toward what one would do to survive, even unto the destruction of a whole civilization, to overcome the hazard we were facing. It was the old adage 'Survival of the fittest." And I was going to survive.

We would form a relationship with some of the inhabitants of this world. They were of the human race but had been born in this place to others who had come here as we had, but died at the hands of those they came to trust. They were allowed to live among the natives but were not a part of their culture. Having discovered these people, they became our source of information that would save our lives.

Lesson one was that this world was a violent and vicious world. You never accomplished anything through kindness or sympathy. The name of the game was to kill and kill in as brutal a manner as you could. Even more demanding was that you killed until your adversary dropped to their knees and surrendered in totality and even then, you may need to kill a few to make your point.

Lesson two, the natives ruled by the lie, and they lied about everything and anything. We learned to not believe anything that was said until we could prove it ourselves. They, the natives, did not know what the word truth meant or how it applied. Oh, they knew what the truth was and how to tell the truth but it took a major move on our part to pry the truth out of them, usually in the form of half a dozen executions. Every contact, every comment was a life-or-death situation and behind that a revolt was building by those we had conquered.

We would be running again and this time from millions of the natives who somehow manage to increase in numbers we had never anticipated. Once we reached sanctuary, we planned our return and final conquest of the beings of this world. Through that, I would become known as Alexander the Great in this world, the second such being that had made history across the universe.

10

Chapter One

In the Beginning

I had to keep running. Nothing else mattered just keep moving, keep running. How long, how long had I been running? Concentrate on running. Don't look back, keep running. Where was I and where was I going? I don't know, just keep running.

Alex found himself running through a forest. He had no idea how he got there. All he knew there was no underbrush so he had to be at a fairly high elevation. The trees were pretty uniform as far as the separation space between them was concerned, and the air was clear and dry. The sky was clear, as clear as he'd ever seen it. It was absolutely silent other than the sound of his feet running over the soft forests floor. All he knew he had to keep running, there was something after him. What it was he had no idea; he could not remember. But he knew he had to keep moving, there was no chance if he stopped and he knew his life was on the line.

He couldn't even remember how he got to where he was at. One moment it was dark and the next moment he's running through this forest aimlessly. He had no idea as to just where he was going to or what he had to do in order to get there. He had to think, he had to come up with something, some idea as to just what the hell is going on.

How long had it been since the last memory of where he was at? Was anybody with him at the time he got to this area, this place? What was he doing here? Where was he going? Why was he doing it in the first place? There was an answer for everything, there had to be. It was all a blank sheet right now. There was nothing there, nothing at all. He needed to think.

He needed to find a sanctuary, a place where he could hold up and think. But for the time being he needed to keep moving. He needed to put the fatigue behind him and drive forward to safety. Whatever was after him meant business and he had to keep moving. How did he know this, he had no idea at all? He knew he had to keep moving. What time was it anyway? A quick look at the sky told him it was high noon. He had lots of time to find a sanctuary.

He had to think. He needed to find a place and find it now. As he scanned ahead of him, he saw a rock outcropping and headed for that. As he rounded the outcropping, he found a small cave. He crawled into the cave and positioned himself so he had a clear view of the entrance. Now he had to start thinking. Now he had to figure out what he was doing here and how he got here.

Everything was all screwed up. He had no idea where he was at. He had no idea how he got here. And he had no idea where he was going. The only thing he did know was his name was Alexander 6 and he had a purpose for being here. Now he had to think. He had to reach into his mind and push all the cloudiness apart and determine what's going on. He knew it was there, he just had to find it.

He started to take an inventory of himself. He found a small backpack that he was wearing. He had a utility belt on with a knife, a compass and a first aid kit. He was wearing a uniform and noted he was also wearing combat boots.

Clearly, he was in the military of some kind. He found no weapons on him other than a knife. He pulled the backpack off and opened it up. Inside he found rations, enough to last him for at least a week. In the bottom of the backpack, he found a small handgun and fifty rounds of ammo. As he looked the gun over, he recognized it. It was a small .32 caliber automatic he had owned for a long time. How the hell did he know that? All he knew was that the gun was familiar and it was his.

Anyway, he had protection. He would be able to cover the entrance of the cave quite well with that weapon. By now fatigue was starting to overcome him and he knew he had to sleep. He crawled back deeper into the cave and to the side in order to get himself out of the view from the mouth of the cave. He then curled up and fell asleep.

Sometime later he woke up and it was dark out. He went back to his backpack and found a lighter and a small candle and lit it. Inside the cave it was quite warm and comfortable. He opened up one of his ration packs and started to eat. It was now time for him to remember. He couldn't wait till morning he had to start now and figure it out, he had to remember.

The next morning as he came out of the cave, he turned to the direction he had come from and started walking. As he started backtracking, moving back through the forest he felt himself moving down as if he was heading down into a valley. As he looked out across the landscape, he saw nothing that was familiar to him. In fact, as far as he could see nothing was familiar.

His night in the cave had gone fitfully. There were times when he slept, times when he lay there trying to remember, and times when a level of fear filled him like nothing he had ever experienced before. All in all, it was not a good night and as he came out of the cave, he could feel the lack of sleep all over his body and the numbness that had seeped into his mind.

He came to a stop and stood there wondering what it was about this place that was familiar to him. He knew this place; he had been here for some time but he still could not pull it all together. Something was blocking him, something so dangerous, so terrible, that he hated even thinking about it.

Had he come here alone or were there others? And if there were others how many? He thought to himself. "Damn, this is going to drive me nuts. I have got to pull myself together and figure this thing out. I simply have no other alternative. I either do that now or I'll never leave this place alive."

He had started walking again trying to follow his tracks from the day before, trying to back track to where he had come from. He stopped again and listened intently for any sound that would be familiar to him or give him an idea as to where he was. He looked around and then walked over to a tree and sat down against it, facing the direction he had come the day before.

Once seated and sure he was alone he got to poking around in his pockets and found a packet of paperwork. As he opened it up, he found his name at the top of each page, five pages in all.

He then started to read. After about ten minutes he had finally finished reading all the papers and then it started to come back to him. He was not just a soldier; he was a captain, the head of a combat unit that had been sent into enemy territory to locate a downed flyer. And now here he was high in these mountains, in a forest, having spent the night in a cave, in a rock outcropping, not knowing what happened to his command.

He finally realized he didn't want to remember what had taken place. The fear, that same fear from yesterday, was starting to well up in him again and he knew he had to overcome it and opened his mind to remember.

The year was 2743. He was part of a larger contingency which came to him as the Starfield Force Unit 943rd. They had entered the contested Ragdelogs territory some three months ago. The purpose was to move into a small star system that his government had laid claim to some one hundred fifty years ago. In just the past year the Ragdelogs had moved into this area in search of natural resources and laid claim to the system. This system consisted of an average size star with eight planets ranging in size from about fifteen miles to forty-three thousand five hundred miles in circumference orbiting the central star.

The occupation by the Ragdelogs was found to be unacceptable by the Starfield United System and as a result the 2743 war started. Starfield Force Unit 943rd was ordered to make a direct attack upon the Ragdelogs forces who had moved into the system and had taken physical control of it. The main purpose was to remove their forces from the system and then prepare for a float battle when they counter attacked.

There was little doubt that the 943rd could and would take the Ragdelog contingency out ether in total or by forcing their surrender. Our best intelligence told the 943rd they outnumbered the enemy almost three to one.

Now Alex was starting to remember. He was in command of a Quick Response Unit made up of two hundred fifty officers and troopers. They had been in on the initial assault of the planets primary defense system and had successfully dislodged the Ragdelog forces and had driven them into a pocket where they had no choice as to whether to surrender or face total annihilation.

Yes, that was it but they had chosen the latter, annihilation and had actually charged out of their fortified bunkers and ran head long into death. At the time the 943rd had seen it as a good omen, but once they had entered the Ragdelog base and saw the condition of the base and the living standards they were surviving under, things started to change.

As the 943rd moved into the Ragdelogs fortifications they found numerous bodies that had been lying around for quite some time. Further investigation showed they had stopped burying their dead at least a full month before the 943rd invaded. Why was that? Why had they stopped burying their dead and why the odd means of death that had been dealt to these bodies?

The Commanding General ordered a detailed investigation into the causes of those deaths and a search of the facility to try and determine why this strange and careless behavior took place as well.

It was two days later when the investigation team met with the general and advised him something far more serious was involved and it was a danger to the entire 943rd. They reported many of the deaths were self-inflicted but almost an equal number were from external attack, the kind of attack that was first of all unbelievable and second was terrifying.

By all they had discovered the entire base complement had gone crazy, and when the 943rd had attacked, they threw themselves at us, not in an attempt to drive us from the planet, but as a means of forcing us to kill them. The team leader then pointed out that many of the dead had been killed by an unknown method that was not of their making. In fact, the team leader had never seen a situation like these, let alone experienced it.

"General, the deaths appeared to be by the same method, but we could not determine just what the hell it was. Also, there appeared to be no pattern in the process of their deaths. That is their bodies their entire bodies were involved in their deaths. They literally died by each and every cell of their bodies dying as if each cell was loaded with explosives and then set off.

But the real nut buster was during the autopsies they discovered that the detonation of each cell was in its own time. By that we mean not all the cells went off at one time. They exploded one after the other throughout their entire body. It must have been excruciating."

The general sat back and looked at the team leader like he was a nut or something and the team leader immediately stated, "General, we have proof of all this and it includes video records of what happened here. Sir, these people died fighting for their lives and in a state of pure and total terror.

"The fact is sir, if we had not attacked this base the entire base would have been completely wiped out to the last person in less than a month. Sir whatever they were fighting was something they could not defend against. It was something that was so terrifying people started to kill themselves whether than face death by the means they were witnessing."

The general sat there and reached up and wiped a line of sweat from his forehead. "Captain, you're telling me this base was under attack before we even got here?"

"Yes sir, it was."

"Then you're telling me this threat still exists and that we are now in the same situation the Ragdelogs were in?"

The team leader was starting to sweat as well. "Yes, sir that is exactly what I am telling you, there is something other than us and the Ragdelogs on this planet that we never knew of or about before. Whatever it is sir it is formidable and terrifying."

The captain no sooner had gotten that out when there was a scream from the trench just outside the general's bunker. Everyone ran outside and looked to their left and saw a trooper lying on the ground. His whole body was withering and sliding all around in the trench. The look on the man's face was probably the most difficult thing to grasp and deal with. His eyes were wide open and literally bulging out of his head. His mouth was wide open but nothing was coming out. He had been stopped right in the middle of a scream.

Just then an object flew between the captain and general and headed down the trench. A trooper came around the corner and the object accelerated and hit the man square in the face as he started to scream. When it hit it was more like a giant water droplet.

When they first saw it, its shape was round and transparent, a clear liquid, and then it hit and splashed across the man's face. This time they had seen it and it was clear that the trooper was not looking at the object but, in their direction, and past the general. Something behind them was seen by that man and then he died.

Everyone turned around but nothing out of the ordinary was there. The general turned to the captain. "I want to see every video you can come up with and I want them right now."

The captain saluted turned and hurried off to collect everything they had found so far. In less than fifteen minutes he was back in the general's bunker and ready to show the videos that had been found.

As the videos ran there was nothing unusual. It was normal base operations as it would be for any military unit from any place throughout the galaxy. Less than three minutes later the camera caught a Ragdelog trooper being hit by a round liquid projectile that was the same as the one they had seen earlier. What stood out was the reaction of the trooper. He was looking at the camera and beyond it. He was seeing something so terrifying he was literally frozen in place and then the round hit him.

They needed to see what that Ragdelog trooper had seen, so they fast forwarded through the videos until they finally came to it. The camera was facing in the right direction. In fact, the man holding the camera was to be the victim. The projectile came down the trench and was just floating along. Just then out behind the projectile the ground was moving and then an object came up out of the ground swung around and literally telescoped itself in the direction of the camera.

At first, they thought it was a mechanical arm that had come out of the ground, but then it started to move closer and higher into the air. It was a living creature. Its main body was rising out of the ground and the neck and head, that's the only way to describe it at this time, moved toward the camera and the man holding it.

Just then a light came from the end of the appendage and the projectile surged ahead toward the trooper and then must have hit its target because the camera fell to the ground.

They immediately started running through the video files as fast as we could when they finally came across a video that must have been hooked up to a stationary camera. That camera had picked up a complete attack from the beginning to the end with the kill.

It took only seconds to realize we were looking at the same incident we had seen on the other tape. It started with an object coming up out of the ground and that object then ejected a projectile, which appeared to come from a mouth or some type of opening. That object or projectile then started moving toward the trench. Behind it came the head and neck of the appendage. And then the main body came up and out of the ground. It was clearly a living thing and it was clearly targeting the trooper.

As the projectile continued toward the trooper, we then saw a beam of light coming from the creature's head to the projectile and then a second one came from the head and went directly to the trooper and he was immediately screaming. It was then we knew some form of an exchange was taking place between the creature and the trooper with the trooper being on the wrong end of the exchange.

Then the projectile came in and hit the man and he went down. It was clear two things had happened to that man. The first was the beam of light from the creature had hit the man and he had reacted. It was like his head was being pulverized by the beam. The second was the projectile hitting him in the face and he immediately went down and his entire body was engulfed in a dance of agony.

The creature then retreated back into the ground. They stood there watching the video, not saying anything. Then the captain pointed at the video screen. "Look, that thing is moving away from the bunker. It's almost like it was swimming through the ground." It then dove and disappeared from sight.

With that the general called a staff meeting of all personnel lieutenants and above. Thirty minutes later the total staff complements of the 943rd were assembled. The general then started the meeting. "Gentlemen I will need each and every one of you to listen up closely. What we are about to cover here involves the survival for this army. No questions will be asked at this time, just pay attention and be ready to move when the order is given.

"When the 943rd took this base, we found a large number of Ragdelog bodies lying all over the base. What was odd to us at the time was that some of the bodies died from self-inflicted wounds and others died in ways and by means that were unknown to us at the time. It was the death of those unknowns that we are here for at this time.

"Gentlemen, those unknowns were killed by a living creature that had attacked the Ragdelogs at least a month before we arrived here. From the time we took this base till two hours ago we had not had any problems or indications of a problem. That is until one of our troopers was killed in the same way the unknowns were killed. Gentlemen we have identified a creature and it is something we have never experienced before. In addition, we do not know at this time whether it is a single creature or one of many.

"What we do know is that this thing lives in the ground and literally swims through the ground, almost like a fish in water. In addition, it appears this creature shoots a projectile that looks like a round droplet of water, but when it hits the victim it literally kills the body cell by cell. In addition, it appears to attack the brain or mind of the victim at the same time. What that does to the victim we have no idea right now.

"We have been pouring over the Ragdelogs videos and records and have determined a number of things at the time they moved into the region. They had built this fortification in a region of the planet that is flat and typical of a plain's layout. For more than a hundred miles to the west, east and north the land is flat and covered with grass. There are few trees or rock outcropping in this region. For lack of a better word, it could be seen as an ocean of grass.

"The only access to an area of land that is higher than this plain is to the south of us. You can see and recognize the forest and mountains in the area. There appears to be a peninsula of rock that reaches out to the fort from the land.

"People, this entire fortress was built as an island in a sea of grass and these creatures literally live and swim in this sea. On top of that, the 943rd has landed right in the middle of it. We have simply replaced the Ragdelogs in this place and it appears we could well be in the same pot they were in.

"As a result, we have contacted the fleet and they are preparing to come in and move the 943rd out of this region and into the mountains. Our analysis tells us these creatures do not inhabit the rocky or mountainous regions and those areas should be safe for us. So, prepare your units for evacuation and redeployment to a region that is one hundred-twenty-miles due east from here.

"Now this is important, no troopers will be permitted to be on their own or alone at any time. Initiate the buddy system and hold them accountable for failing to maintain that orientation. Every single Ragdelog death was found to be a lone trooper either standing guard or doing some duty on their own. The one troop we lost was alone as was the second. That will no longer be permitted.

"All right move out and prepare to redeploy in two hours."

So, there it was. We had discovered what had taken place at this base and we now were going to abandon it for safer ground in the mountains. Who would have thought there were creatures living on this planet let alone creatures that swam through the ground like a fish and were as deadly as anything we had ever met before?

Chapter Two

The Lost Command

Alex sat there looking out onto the plains and remembering what had happened. Yet he still needed to come up with the actual move and then the detail he was working when he ended up here, high in this mountain range running for his life.

Slowly each and every detail of these past two months came into focus for him. The general had just ordered the redeployment into the mountains to the east and the space fleet was working its way back into the region of the planet to assist in the move.

It would be impossible to make that move on land. They would have to be air lifted out of the plain's location and to the mountains, there was no other choice. The entire battle unit of the 943rd had assembled in the jump off point waiting for the first of the air transports to drop in and load up. It was then when a lookout noted movement in the areas outside the base and on all sides of the fortification.

As the general looked the situation over, he could see the creatures rolling in the plains. It was one of those things when witnessed that was amazing to a person seeing it for the first time. It made him think of whales as they breach the surface of the ocean and then dive for the depths. There had to be at least fifty of the creatures rolling and breaching the surface of the plains at that time.

It was stupefying to say the least. These things had to be as dense as steel if not denser in order to move through the ground in that way. It was the same ground he was standing on and yet we could not penetrate it without a shovel or some other digging device. Yet, there they were breaching and rolling just as if it was water.

The captain turned to the general. "Sir, if that land out there is the same as this land in here then why are they not swimming through this area as well?"

The general looked at the captain and then his staff team. "That is one damn hell of a question. Why haven't we thought of that before now? That could mean the difference between survival and total defeat."

He then turned and looked back out toward the rolling creatures and then back to his staff. "Well, let's find an answer and find it right now. Why the hell are they staying out there when they could just as well swim right through this place and wipe out the whole of us out in minutes?"

The major jumped up on the berm of the trenches and took a quick look around. As he jumped back into the trench a liquid ball flew just over his head and landed on the ground not fifteen feet from him. It didn't break but sat there not moving or showing any indication of activity.

The general pointed at the ball. "Get that thing and contain it in something but don't touch it with your hands or any part of your body."

The ball was collected and sent off to be analyzed by their science unit. It was at this time that the first of the air support units started to arrive. They were circling the base and preparing to land when the creatures outside the base started shooting liquid balls at the aircraft.

The lead craft was coming in for a landing took a direct hit from several balls and started to come apart, as if someone was cutting all its joints and seams with a cutting torch. The ship never made it to the base. It fell about three hundred feet from the base proper and within seconds the creatures were on the craft and buried it before anyone could get out.

The general turned to the major. "Major what did you see while you were on top of the berm?"

"Sir I noted there appear to be several rocky outcroppings within the base proper. As I scan the plains beyond here, I could see several locations where there are rock outcroppings and the creatures generally stay away from those areas. I would say sir, based on that observation this is a fairly safe location for us."

The general stood there and started to nod his head. "That would explain much of what was going on here. Look the Ragdelogs set this base up taking advantage of the natural fortifications that were here in this area. This gave them a good field of fire on anything that approached the base by land. It also gave them strong points that could withstand artillery hits. They did a good job setting up for us. The problem was they failed to set up for the creatures and this place then became a trap, a trap we are now in."

He then turned to his staff in charge of engineering. "Gentlemen this is what I want. I want a geo-dome built over this base. Second, I want piling driven into the ground till they hit bedrock. If we're going to be trapped here, we might as well make it safe. How long will it take you?"

The lead officer stood there a minute looking the base area over. "Sir we can complete the job in four days. Not only can we put the dome in, but we can make it retractable so that air craft can drop in as well. That is if they can get by the creatures and their liquid balls."

The general stood there and nodded his head. "All right get with it, but take it easy and make sure no one gets killed by those things during the construction work. Understood?"

Within three hours aircraft dropped the needed materials and supplies and the engineers set to work. The laser diggers started digging the piling holes. Because of the amount of bedrock in the area of the base they were able to complete the piling holes in less than ten hours.

Next, they placed the steel forms and then the concrete was poured and the foundation was completed by midday the next day. It was time to start the dome and finish the project. These domes come in six x six panels and are assembled one layer or row at a time with an angle built into them so that the final panel, when placed in the remaining hole, fit perfectly.

By late the third day the final panel was bolted into place and the dome was secured. The material of this system can withstand a direct hit by most any weapons system out there today. The 943rd was holed up and safe from further attacks by the creatures.

During this time the fleet had been conducting surveys of the region to try to determine the numbers and makeup of the indigenous life forms on the planet. Any attempt to attack and kill the swimming creatures failed. They were just too dense for the weapons to penetrate and kill them. Some other form of attack needed to be developed.

Now they had to figure a way out of that area. They were protected from the creatures, but they could not stay forever. They had to move out of that place and so they went to work figuring how to get out of the plains and up into the mountain regions.

However, there was one problem and that was the question of the types of life systems that could or would be living in the high country. It was logical to think if there were life forms in the plains then there were in the high countries as well.

The first decision was that they would construct a tunnel of some type. It would have to be an armored tunnel and one that was far denser than the creatures they were dealing with. The question that needed to be answered was what was the density of the creature? The fleet scientists set to work figuring that out. They determined the density of the ground makeup on the planet. Then they took measurements of the creature movements through the ground and with that they were able to make an educated guess as to the creature's density.

The resulting tunnel system was rated at twice the density of the estimate of the creatures. The system started to arrive at the base and it was laid across the land from the base to the start of the mountains. They literally floated the tunnel across the land. The creatures seemed oblivious to the tunnel and in fact seemed to avoid it completely.

After six weeks the system was completed and the first vanguard of troopers moved through the tunnel to the high ground and set up a fire base at that location. They advanced into the region in full expectation of some kind of attack waiting for them. None came when they arrived on the upper regions. The main base remained occupied by the base command while the rest of the 943rd moved across the low lands and into the mountain regions.

Up to this point the 943rd had successfully faced and dealt with the hazards that were discovered around the base. Now they needed to take that warning and take care and be aware of any further dangers they may discovered in the coming days. They would not have to wait long.

This small planet, in this out of the way location of the Starfield United System was actually in an area where little or no exploration had been carried out. The Starfield United System had grown and expanded so fast it out grew its resources for carrying out an in-depth exploration of all that it controlled. Never the less, when the Ragdelogs made a move to take this system from us we had to respond and so we were now in the thick of it.

Who knew what we would find when we arrived at this system? The Ragdelogs didn't and it cost them everything. We were fortunate enough to be the second to come here and so it gave us an advantage, one that would help us survive, just barely.

It was at this time a small reconnaissance aircraft came up missing while on a flight into the unknown region of the planet we were preparing to enter. My quick response unit, Fire Response Unit Seven, was directed to move into the region, in Force, find where the craft went down and retrieve the pilot, dead or alive.

That morning we loaded up and started out in the direction of the last know contact with the craft. I had two hundred fifty troopers in the Company, including my second in command and unit sergeants. The best guess information on the location of the craft was ten miles due east of the base and about half way up the mountain range we were heading into.

Yeah, I was starting to remember now. Lieutenant Steel, my second in command, stood there by me as the lead SPU (Scout Patrol Unit) started out ahead of the Company. "Captain, you think we'll find him alive?"

I was busy thinking about what had happened in the valley and had not considered the issue as to whether the pilot was alive or not. "That Lieutenant is not the issue. The general wants the pilot found and recovered, dead or alive. Either way we are to recover him."

"I understand sir, but with all that took place down below and us heading into an area where we have no idea as to what is out there, I thought maybe we were taking on more than we're prepared for." He was earnest and I could tell rather uneasy with the whole assignment.

This seemed odd to me because this man never gave you any indication, he was fearful or doubted any assignment given him or the Company. I turned to Brad and looked at him. "Brad is there something wrong? Look, the general's orders were to go into that region in force and you know what that means?"

"Yeah, Captain I do, but I also saw what those things in the valley could do and I have this damned feeling we're walking into the wrong end of a gun barrel." He was clearly concerned but I could see he was also prepared. He had that look about him I was accustomed to and it told me Brad would do what he needed to do and do it well.

Twenty minutes before we set out, the general walked up to me. "Alex, you take care out there, hear me? Expect just about anything and anticipate at all times. If this planet can produce creatures like those down below, then it can create just about anything. So, pay attention and if things look bad, pull back. Understood?"

I looked in the general's eyes and I could see his concern. We were responding to a direct order from the fleet command. Someone had to go out and locate the pilot and bring him back. That was our job and so we had to go. In all our wildest dreams, hell could never be as bad.

At nine hundred hours, the point team moved out of the base and headed due east, in the direction of the pilot's personal locator signal. We had formed up in lines of two on both sides of the trail and were followed up by the rear-guard unit.

A quick response unit such as this is a self-contained unit. We carry enough fire power to handle just about anything we come up against. Units of this type have been known to take on a full battalion and reduce it to nothing but bodies. We carry the best of communications equipment, weaponry, medical supplies, and food. We can survive in any environment for no less than four weeks and if need be, live off the land for much longer. Bottom line, we are the best of the best.

Things were nominal during the first five miles. We had seen no signs of activity above or below us on the trails. There were numerous trails cutting all over the place but they appeared to have little or no activity on them. Yes, trails indicate something has made them and we knew that there was animal life on this planet, so the fact there were lots of trails was nothing to be concerned about.

What was concerning was the fact we were seeing no animal activity at all.

In fact, other than the sound of two hundred fifty men moving along the trails, there was nothing but dead silence. At the five and a half miles mark the point unit called a halt to our advancement. Sergeant Todd came on line and advised they were observing movement three hundred yards ahead and above the trail line. I gave the order to arm weapons at which point you could hear the bolts dropping all along the line.

We were currently in our battle line with our troops moving by twos about four hundred feet long. I gave the order to move into combat formation at which time the company broke into two equal forces and formed up in a "V" formation off of the patrol unit's lead position. The rear guard then set up as a rear observation line from the ends of the two lines forming the "V".

From that formation each troop had a field of fire that was roughly ninety degrees from dead ahead to either the left or right depending on which wing of the "V" they were on. Under coordinated fire we could literally level the forest for several hundred yards in both frontal directions. A portion of the "V" could be reversed and carry out the same fire configuration to the rear as well.

In addition, we could fall back into a defensive diamond formation and cover the entirety of our perimeter with a withering level of fire power. We looked in good shape at this time and I gave the go ahead to move out and continue our advancement toward the beacon signal area.

The underbrush in the forest for this area was not a problem. The ground was uniform and firm and made for good footing. The underbrush in the area was equally spread out on the forest floor and averaged around two feet in height. Overall, the ability to move and observe was good.

It was another half mile before we came to stop again, but this time nothing came from Sergeant Todd. I waited and then called Todd. "Command to Todd?"

Nothing, I looked at Brad and then called the point patrol again. "Command to Todd?"

There was dead silence. I was positioned at the point of the "V" and therefore had a clear field of vision ahead of me. The Patrol should have been just a hundred feet out ahead of us but I could see nothing. No movement or anything to tell me where they were.

Just then the left flank observed movement to our left and ahead of us. Whatever it maybe it was coming directly at us. Just then we saw a trooper coming toward us through the brush, it was Sergeant Todd. He was covered in blood and his weapon was missing. As he came closer, we could see the reason for the missing weapon was the fact that his arm was missing as well. His eyes were glassy and he was trying to speak but nothing came out, that is nothing recognizable.

As he approached, he dropped to his knees about ten yards from me and then dropped face first to the ground. It was then I saw the branch or vine that was wrapped around his neck. As soon as he fell the vine came loose and shot across the ground and joined up with one of the bushes that were all over the place.

I reached back and grabbed Brad. "Brad, it's the plants, the bushes. Pass this down the line I want ever other man to face into the formation and prepare flame throwers. At my signal I want all the brush within fifty yards of us burned completely.

Tell everyone to stick with their training and clear the underbrush.

The word was passed and everyone maneuvered into position. I then gave the order and everyone lit up at once. The plants responded just as fast and shot vines out grabbing a number of troops and dragging them out of line and coiling around them and dragging them underground screaming and kicking all the way.

It was a short battle but it cleared the bushes away from our position for forty to fifty yards all around us. Casualty reports came in at seventeen lost. We were all in a state of shock after seeing and experiencing this thing. I don't know if I was the first but it then dawned on me that it was the plants of this world that were the hazard to us, not the animals. The plants were intelligent and aggressive.

As I thought about it, I realized those creatures in the valley would fit that description perfectly. They had a relationship with the ground and were part of it and as a result they could move through it at will. I then realized they did not actually move but in fact grew through the ground at an accelerated rate which made them appear to be floating or swimming through the ground.

I made contact with the base and asked for the general. He came on line and I reported our situation and then explained what we had come up against. "General, their plants sir, the things in the valley, the creatures, they were moving because they could grow so fast, they looked like they were swimming. They would leave their old roots behind and those would decompose almost immediately and go back into the soil. Sir the whole of the ground is aggressive in this place and we've walked right into it."

There was a long silence and then he came back. "All right Alex we have you on that and we think you're right. Now we need you to reverse your position and return to the base as soon as you can, got that?"

"Yes, sir received and understood. We will start our return now." I was not sure just how we were going to do it but we needed to move and move now. The plants were not going to wait forever before coming back at us.

I gave the order to reverse and head back for the main base. It was then that Brad looked up into the trees and discovered they, the trees, were sending vines down on top of us. They almost nailed us when we cut loose on them with the flame throwers. A few of the troops panicked but for the most part they held their position and kept firing.

I then caught sight of the brush starting to reach out toward us and ordered half the command to redirect its fire on the brush. At this rate we could keep the firing going until we reached the main base. What I didn't count on was the roots of the trees. It started with troopers suddenly dropping out of sight. I then realized they were coming in under us and taking people out, literally dragging them underground to their death.

I yelled over at Brad. "Brad, hit the trees, the trunks with hard weapons. Got me?"

He waved his hand and started grabbing men and redirecting their fire. The rounds started going in on the trees. As they hit, we could hear screams of pain and then we saw the blood running out of them. I got back on the line to command. "Command you receiving me?"

"That's affirmative." They responded.

"Are you getting the telemetry?"

"Again, that is affirmative."

"General you need to look at the trees. Sir they're more than just alive, they are intelligent beings and they bleed when we hit them. Sir you're in trouble there if you don't clear every tree within several hundred yards of the base out. Kill them sir, every one of them." I knew he had to take action and do it now if they were to going to survive.

I also knew I needed to act and act aggressively so that we could get back to the base, but things were starting to really turn against us here.

By this time, I had lost maybe twenty percent of my command. The ground was literally eating them up one and two at a time. People were starting to panic and our command control was fragmenting.

It was then that I saw the sky light up to the east. The General had called in the heavy guns from the fleet and they were raking the forest around the base and killing everything and anything within a mile of the base. We continued to fight our way toward the base when I saw the fleet was now clearing a trail for us back to the base.

They had made it to almost two hundred yards from us when all hell cut loose. Everything came alive all at once. The ground literally erupted with roots and vines as they impaled and grabbed troops all along the front line. They were dragging them into the ground, some being torn apart as they were ripped off their feet and taken.

I don't blame my guys one bit; it was a hopeless situation and so they broke. The fact was so did Brad and so did I. We were running for our lives and the plants were just decimating us. What else could we have done but run and run as hard as we could.

The problem was, no matter where we ran, we were running into more trees and brush and more death. I don't know, I remember Brad being there with me but I can't remember when he was not there. I didn't hear him or see him anywhere and so I ran. I started to run up the mountain and I kept going up until I came to the outcrop and then I headed for cover.

I now realize I had entered a part of the mountain that was heavy in rocky terrain. It was an area where the plants couldn't grow and as a result, I was safe for the time being. That is until I walked down from that location and finally sat down against a tree. That froze me right in my place. I had to move and move now, but I did not want it to appear I was in a panic. Just get up and quietly move back around and up into the rocky area. Funny, it let me go.

I sat down against a rock and stared back down the mountain toward where my command had been. A whole Company, two hundred fifty officers and troops of a Quick Strike unit wiped out in a matter of minutes. As far as I knew I was the lone survivor and I would have to face the inquisition that was to follow, that is if I ever got back to the base.

The base, I looked back to the southwest and saw a haze of clouds and dust hanging over where the base was at. There were periodic bursts of cannon fire from the fleet overhead, but other than that it appeared to be quiet down there. I needed to do something besides sitting here and so I started to plan.

I went over in my mind what had happened the day before realizing we had walked dead on into a trap. Who would have thought the primary life force on this planet were the plants? It was obvious they were predatory and they had some form of a mental process. Otherwise, they couldn't have carried out the actions they did in the process of destroying my command.

The one thing that was in our favor was that plants are stationary and they have no means of transportation or getting from point "A" to point "B".

However, there was still the problem of the ground. They ruled the ground. I mean they controlled all that went on underneath us, under the surface of the planet. That was obvious by the actions of the roots and smaller plants around us.

That brought up another issue, where was their mental capacity located, in the above ground portion of the plant or below ground. If it was above ground then every plant that is killed above ground kills the mental capabilities of that plant. On the other hand, if the mental capacity was underground then taking out the above ground did nothing to mitigate the actions of the plant overall.

Next, what about there being a central mental control system for a large area of the planet which controlled any number of plants over that area?

God, this could go on indefinitely. Yet, there was the bleeding? When the trees were hit with gun fire they bled. Come to think of it they also screamed. Screamed? They vocalized and that meant communications. It also meant they could feel pain, a lot of pain.

That brought me back to the lowlands and the large creature moving around the Ragdelog base. We had realized they were not moving through the ground like they were swimming but in fact were growing through the ground. They had roots and they were growing those roots which in turn pulled their body around through the ground. So, if they could move like that, why not the trees?

I needed to get the hell back down there and back to the base. This thing was far more complex and dangerous than anyone had any understanding of. It meant going down and through the trees and right then and there I had no idea how I was going to do it, but I had to and it had to be now before it was too late.

We had come here to remove the Ragdelogs from our region of space and now that it had been done, it was time for us to leave this place and leave it now. The question was would they let us? Would they give us the freedom to move around them in any force or numbers of people? I doubted that and knew the answer would not be favorable.

Chapter Three

Rebuilding the Command

I knew I had to get back to the base, but between me and the base was a whole forest of danger, plants that were ready to kill me on sight. My problem was getting past them and home in a reasonable time frame.

I stood up and started to look around. The area I had run into was heavy with rock outcroppings and had few plants of any kind. As I stood there, I looked down at the tree I had first sat down at and I got to thinking. When I sat down it took no action against me, why?

I walked back down to the tree and stood there looking at it and the ground around it. I scraped my shoe toe across the ground and after a few scrapes I hit rock. I walked over to the tree and again scraped the top soil away and found rock. The tree had grown in a break or crack in the overall rock structure in this area. If it had a strong root system it was down deep and not a threat to me.

I pulled my knife and stepped up to the trunk and pushed the blade into the tree all the way through the bark and into the wood. Nothing, not a spot of blood and not any kind of a reaction, it was just a tree and nothing more. That brought up more questions than I had answers for. That always seems to be the way things go. You solve one question and four more crop up. Strange, it was a lone tree separated from the main forest and showing no signs of intelligence or pain reaction. It was just a tree.

I then started to look around the general area. That part of the mountain was more rock than anything else. I looked along the ridge above me and saw that it ran clear across the area in both directions. I could move up on to that ridge and move across until I was over the main base location.

My next task would be to find a means of getting down and back to the base. I guess I would have to wait till I got that far before I dealt with the issue. Yet, there was something else I needed to do before leaving this area and that was to go down and see if I could locate any of my command. It was a risk, but one I felt I had to take.

Damn, I hated the idea of doing that, but if I had anyone left, I had to find them and bring them back. I did a check of my equipment and then looked down the hill toward the wooded area. As I stood there looking it over, I realized there was no undergrowth at all. The wooded area was open and consisted solely of trees and nothing else, not even grass.

The next thing that came to me was that each tree was spaced almost the same distance from every other tree. I would say there was around six to ten feet between trees making it an easy area to move through. Still, I had that gut feeling with that much space about anything could be waiting for me.

It was then I made a decision that if asked later on, I would not be able to explain why I chose that route or process of moving through the trees. I decided I wanted to stay as close to the trees as possible and only move across open areas when I moved from tree to tree. In a nut shell I was going to be a tree hugger.

I worked my way down to the tree line and then stopped and watched for a few minutes. What I was looking for was any sign of my command such as equipment, clothing, or people lying among the trees. After a few minutes I realized there was nothing there, no sign of anyone.

Finally, I decided to take the step that would determine whether I was ever going to get home. I walked directly over to the nearest tree and stood there beside it, again watching for any reaction to my presence or for any telltale objects that would give me any idea as to what happened to my command.

I stood there waiting and listening, there was nothing, just a dead silence in every direction. Damn, it was like a chess game. I stood there looking at the four closest trees, trying to determine which one I would advance to. Was one any better or safer than the others?

I finally took the step and moved directly downhill to the next tree. Again, nothing and again I stood there watching and listening for anything out of the ordinary or that would warn me of a danger.

I continued this process for the next fifteen minutes moving from one tree to the next then stopping and looking and listening. It was dead calm everywhere I looked and at every tree I moved to. I was getting ready to make my next jump when something caught my eye off to my left. I stood still looking that way and then I saw it again. It was a foot, one foot sticking out from behind a tree and it was moving.

The first thing to hit my mind was "Fish bait" was I looking at a lure placed there to draw me in and then ending up falling into a trap. I stood there watching that foot for I don't know how long and all it did was sit there and move back and forth in the same spot.

Au, screw it anyway, they either take me or they don't, but I have to check this out and make sure this person is alright. I moved over two trees until I was uphill from the tree in question. I again stood there watching and then moved down to the tree and stood there on the opposite side from the foot. I slowly moved around the tree and as I did, I then saw a leg and then the hips and then Brad. He was sitting there looking down the hill into the trees. The only thing moving was his right foot.

I kneeled down beside him and reached out and put my hand on his right shoulder and shook him. He sat there a minute and then slowly turned his head toward me and looked up at me.

His eyes were damn near dead. They were dull and didn't seem to see or respond to anything. I stayed there by him waiting for a response. God only knows how long he had been sitting there, and while there seeing whatever he saw down below him.

I looked down the hill in the direction he was looking and after a few seconds I could see the ground rolling. Everywhere you looked between the trees down there the ground was rolling and then I saw a hand come up out of the ground for a second and then it rolled back down under the ground. Over to the left I saw a leg roll up out of the ground and then disappear back into the soil.

I turned around and sat down beside Brad and leaned back against the tree and sat there watching. There was my command in that forest of trees being turned and rolled around like so many potatoes in a pealing machine. It was mesmerizing to say the least.

Once you became used to looking at the scene before you it was clear there were a lot of bodies down there in that ground. They were being rolled and moved around, up and out of the ground and then being pulled back down into the ground continuously. Why I had no idea, but there were hundreds of them. The ground there before us was a madhouse of activity with a combination of soil, roots, and human bodies being turned, rolled, and tossed in a never-ending process.

Brad reached over and took my arm. "I've been watching the process all morning and slowly but surely all their equipment and clothing has been removed from them and they then sunk out of sight. Only their equipment and clothing are then left on the surface."

He went quiet again and sat there. "Damn I don't want that to happen to me."

I looked at him, "You all right?"

He sat there for maybe thirty seconds and then looked at me. "Yeah, I'll be all right. Just scared and not really knowing what happened. Do you know what happened down there?"

"Not really. I just know the forest came alive and kicked our asses all over the mountains." I sat there looking at the scene below us.

"Yeah, whatever it is, it really did kick our asses. Now what?" He was turned toward me again looking right at me.

"Now what?"

He looked back down the hill again. "I think we need to get back to the base and get ready to come back and deal with this thing whatever it is."

That set me back and I looked at him. He must have seen it in my face and eyes. "No Captain, I'm not crazy, I'm pissed off. We got the hell kicked out of us yesterday and we deserved it. But that doesn't change the fact I want to get even. We should have seen it in the low lands when those creatures appeared. We see it now, but we should have seen it early on and we didn't.

"We accept plants as some kind of food base and not a live thinking organism. Well, they are and we need to deal with it. Whatever we do, before we leave this place, we are going to let them know who the more superior beings are and they should pray we never return. The fact is, I would prefer we left this place with every living plant burned to a hundred feet below the ground."

One thing I knew right then and there was Brad was not in too bad a shape. He had made it through and was mad as hell, and quite frankly I needed him that way. I knew if we were going to make it back to the base, I needed him to be on top of everything and mad as hell. The madder the better as long as he kept thinking as well, he still needed to be aware and ready for whatever may come.

Finally, I stood up and he came up to his feet. We stood there looking down at the trees below us. "Look we're not going to be able to go down through there. I have been looking the upper ridge over and I think we can move along that ridge until we're over the main base and then move on down from there. If we're lucky the fleet may have burned away most of the plant life from the ridge down to the base."

He was nodding his head and looking up at the ridge as well. "Yeah, I think you've got something there. At least we'll not have to fight our way all along that area and that should give us about five miles of easy movement before we have to face the descent."

He was thinking now and that gave me the confidence to move out and head for the ridge. As we moved around the tree Brad grabbed my arm and pulled me back. He then pointed over to our right at about a forty-five-degree angle. "Captain there is something over there. I saw something moving there just a second ago."

I moved back behind the tree and then looked around in the direction he was pointing. There was nothing and I was just getting ready to say something when a movement caught my eye. "Yeah, there it was over by the tree."

Brad moved around to the upper side of our tree and then moved away and up the hill to the next tree. We were set to make the move on that tree when I saw the movement again and then he came out from behind the tree. "Captain is that you?"

It was the missing second point man, Sergeant Dent, "Hey Sergeant, over here."

He came running over to my position while Brad moved back down to where we were at, "Dent, how the hell where you able to get up here anyway?"

"Not sure Captain all I know is all hell busted loose and next thing I know is I'm here and I can't find anyone. Last I saw of my unit they were overrun by a bunch of roots. Roots damn-it, how could that be?" He looked like hell, but seemed to be just fine.

I stood there looking at the other two. All right now we're three and that makes the odds better for us. "Sergeant, you have a weapon?"

He looked at himself and then patted his holster. "Yeah, I've got my sidearm and that's all I need."

Finally, I felt like I needed to move out and then pointed to the east. "I think I want to move along this line above the tree line down there and see if we come across any others in that direction. If the three of us made it up here there may be others who did the same."

Brad was looking west. "Captain what about in that direction as well. Think there could be any that made it up out there?"

"Yeah, there sure as hell could have been." I turned and looked the same direction. "Look I don't want us to split up so let's take a run out that way, to the east, for a few hundred yards and if we don't find anyone we can then turn back and head for the base."

We set out to the east. Sergeant Dent took the point without being asked and we moved off cautiously looking for survivors. We had gone maybe a hundred feet when we saw our first body. This one had made it out of the trees below but had been so badly injured he died after getting clear of the trees below.

We looked around and saw a number of loose rocks over at the base of a small cliff. We moved the trooper over to that location and covered him with rocks. We marked the grave for later recovery and then move out going east again.

The terrain remains fairly even as we moved east except the ridge above us moved down ahead of us and would eventually pinch us off and force us back down into the tree line below us, a place we didn't want to go. We were just getting ready to turn around when Sergeant Dent signaled a stop and then pointed to our left.

There just thirty feet down from us was another body, but this time the trooper rose up and saw us and jumped to his feet and ran to meet us. He was one of our radio men and he still had his system with him. He had not used it since the battle but said that it still worked.

We all moved back up the hill and further away from the tree line and then settled down. The Trooper fired the radio up and I made the call to the base. "Fire Response Unit Seven to Alpha Base, come in."

There was silence and I repeated the call a second time. This time there was a response. "Fire Response Seven where are you?"

This was it and I knew I had to tell them what had happened. "Base, there are four of us at this time. We are east of the base and above the main tree line at the base of the ridge. We are preparing to move west on the ridge to a point over the base and then move down into the tree line and hopefully on through to the base, over."

"Fire Response Seven who is this?

I took a deep breath. "Base this is Captain Alexander."

There was a pause again and then the general came back. "Alex what is your condition at this time?"

I felt a hard knot form in my gut and then started my report. "General as far as I know my entire command has been wiped out except for myself, Lieutenant Steel, and Sergeant Dent and Trooper Adams. We plan on heading west at this time and looking for any other survivors on the way to our drop off point where we plan to head down to the base.

There was a pause and the general came back. "All right Alex you let us know when you're a mile east of the drop off point and we will have the fleet drop a few rounds into that area to clear out the rest of the trees and undergrowth so you can get through. Got that?"

"Loud and clear sir, we're heading out at this time. I'll call when we're ready for the cover rounds."

I was feeling much better by this time and had a good feeling about this whole mess.

We all sat there for a few minutes longer just to give ourselves time to ramp up for the run that was ahead of us. I didn't anticipate too much of a problem from here to the five-mile point when we reached that position it placed us up above the main base. From then on it was anyone's guess as to what would be waiting for us.

Sergeant Dent took the point again and Brad took rear cover and we headed out. We returned the way we came and reached our original jump off point and then continued on heading into the unknown. The key to this whole thing was to stay above the main tree line and away from any undergrowth. At the same time, we were watching for additional survivors.

We hadn't gone fifty yards when we spotted the next trooper sitting at the base of a tree. His left leg was gone at the knee and he had lost a lot of blood but had managed to stop the bleeding and was still alive. We put together a gurney and Trooper Adam and I took the job of carrying the injured troop and set out again.

We kept up a constant dialog going so that if anyone was nearby, they would hear us and let us know they were there. This looked like it could turn into a major rescue mission instead of a survival mission.

We knew we had around five miles to go in this upper region as we followed the rocky ridge above us. In that distance there had to be more waiting for someone to find them and bring them home.

Having thought that, we found our next trooper, he was in good shape but was clearly out of it. The guy was scared crazy and we had to give him a sedative before we started to move out again. We put the new man on the gurney with Trooper Adams and then set out again. The key to this whole thing was to keep moving and make sure everyone had something to do. Can't give them any time to think about what had happened and what was coming. We had to keep moving and looking.

It took us eight hours to go the four or five miles to the end of the ridge run. In that time, we collected another fifteen troopers, some fully armed and other missing everything including their pack and belts. Out of a two hundred fifty-man regiment we had twenty-one left.

We were now faced with the issue of making the next run down the mountain to the base. I could see from the top of the ridge line the strip of forest that had been burned to the main base. The best I could estimate we still have around a hundred to two hundred yards of trees between us and the fire lane that had been cut.

I got on the radio to the base and reported to the general where we were at and we would be ready to head down the mountain at any time. It was decided to wait it out till the next morning and then make a run for it. That would give us time to rest and prepare ourselves. In addition, the general could get together with the fleet and set up a fire assignment to clear out the rest of the forest between us and the fire lane we were heading for.

I took Lieutenant Steel, Brad, aside and started to work up our primary assault plan. He had collected a complete inventory of the hardware the troops had. At the same time Sergeant Dent had the troops together and was working them into a formal organization. I knew he would have it all done by morning and we would have a well-organized team ready to head out.

That night, before sun down, I went over to the men and sat down with them. They needed to know how I felt and what was coming. "Guys, tomorrow is going to be one of the hardest days we will ever face. I know what you're all thinking about and the truth is not one of us is not thinking of tomorrow. The bottom line is we don't have any choice in the matter we have to go for it.

"I have talked to the general and they are working up a barrage for us to try and take out the rest of the trees and underbrush between here and the camp. If they can do the same thing they did before then we should have no problem getting through to the base.

"Now I need you to understand we are still facing an unknown here. Just because they take out the rest of the plant life between here and the base does not mean they will remove the hazard to us. It could just as well increase the hazard; we just don't know. So, I want you to get a good night's rest. Take your time and sleep as long as you want. We will not move out until after the barrage and then it will only be when we're ready.

"Prepare yourselves accordingly and remember that we all go together. If anyone ops to stay behind, well you stay behind. We're going and that's it, so get yourselves ready and plan on a major assault action in the process. We have several wounded and we will not leave them, they are coming with us so plan your actions accordingly.

"Sergeant Dent will head up the point unit and Lieutenant Steel will head up the rear guard. The rest of us will move the wounded and cover our flanks at the same time. Now listen up, the real danger is the ground. Do not stand in any one spot for any period of time and I'm talking seconds not minutes. Once we move, we keep moving.

If anyone goes down help them up and keep them moving. If they go down and will not respond to your prodding them then you leave them and keep moving. Look we do not want to see anyone left behind so each of you must develop a mind set to keep moving. If you stop and someone must stop to help, you have placed that person in jeopardy along with you. Got me?"

Everyone was nodding their heads. These were good men and they have been in hard spots before and knew what was at stake. They had seen some rather unbelievable things happen over the last thirty hours and I can understand if they're a little shell shocked by this time. Still, they had to understand what was at stake and the fact they either moved or they died.

That evening I spent about forty-five minutes with the general working up the barrage action in the morning. It was determined for us it would be best if we were on top of the ridge line when the barrage took place. If it was successful, we would have all the time in the world to make the run down to the base. If not, then the call was mine and mine alone.

Chapter Four

The 943rd Falls

The following morning it was warm and clear which gave us a clear view of the area we would be crossing and the valley below. From the ridge line I could see the base and most of the forest area above that. I would estimate we had maybe one or two hundred yards of forest that needed to be flattened before we made the run. If they couldn't do that then I had a decision that needed to be made.

I sat there looking down on the base when it came to me there was something wrong, something did not look right. I reached over to Lieutenant Steel. "Lieutenant, give me your binoculars."

As Brad handed his binoculars to me. "What do you see Captain, is there something wrong?"

"Brad I'm not sure but things do not look right down at the base, I need to take a closer look at it.

As I brought the binoculars to my eyes and adjusted them so I could get a clear view I focused in on the base I saw something that took my breath away. There was a clear view all right, the only problem was it was covered with roots, a mass of moving crawling roots, the base had fallen.

I leaned back and looked over at Brad. "We lost the base. We're here on this planet all by ourselves."

Brad stood up and turned facing in the direction of the base. That's impossible. There is no way they could take that base, no way at all.

"Well Brad they did, the place is crawling with roots and I see no one else moving around out there. It's clear to me we have lost the base and everybody on its. Our only out now is to contact the fleet and report to the admiral about the base and our situation." I was trying to maintain control of myself while talking to Brad. I didn't want my men to hear there was a problem.

I turned to my radioman and directed him to make contact with the fleet, I needed to talk to the admiral immediately. I had little doubt, the general was no longer in control of the base. I know that I talked to the general on the radio but it could be he was under the control of the plants. Whatever the situation is we can no longer return to the base.

That moment the radioman advised me. "Sir I have the Admiral online."

I took the mic from the radioman's hand, keyed it. "Admiral this is Captain Alexander of Fire Response Unit Seven. Sir it appears the base has been taken over by the plants and we are no longer able to return to that location."

There was a long pause before the admiral got back to me. I had been sitting there looking down at the base wondering what had happened. Just then the admiral came on the line. "Captain we lost contact with the base three hours ago. We have tried time and again to regain contact but there are no answers. The best we can figure is that the base fell sometime in the four hours prior to our last attempt to contact them. Give me your coordinates at this time.

I pulled out my compass and map and set up to determine our location by map coordinates. I then advised the admiral. "Admiral we are about four and a half miles south of the base on the rocky ridge running east and west above the tree line. Refer to map coordinates P471 alpha 6.

The fleet operator came back online. "Fire Response Unit Seven, be advised the fleet will reposition itself to fire directly on the base and clear it of any root occupation. The fleet will then adjust its firing and take out the wooded area just north of the ridge and your position. You have ten minutes to find cover and to remain there until notified."

That sounded a little drastic to me. "Admiral, are you sure the base is completely wiped out and none of our people are left there?"

There was a pause and then he came back. "Captain from our position we have been able to determine a number of personnel from the 943rd have pulled back out to the Ragdelog base in the valley and are holding out there. They advise that the base is totally overrun by root systems and anyone there has been consumed by the system, including the general."

"Sir, are they sure the general was taken, I talked to him this morning just before discovering the takeover and he sounded fine to me. Sir is there any way to confirm what has happened on that base?"

I was becoming more confused every minute until the Admiral finally came back on line and advised. "Captain, we understand the situation you're in. So, maybe we need to fill you in on just what is going on."

Finally, it sounded like something was going to happen that would bring some clarity to our situation. "That sir would be greatly appreciated."

He came on line and started to brief us. "Gentlemen, three days ago when you set out on your mission to locate and recover a downed pilot east of the base the fleet was monitoring the actions of your unit and those of the base.

"As your unit moved east from the base, we noted the activity within the trees around your unit and they were acting just like an intelligently led military force. At that same time, we discovered a second action was starting back at the base itself. The plants in that area were forming up and a coordinated assault started on the base at the same moment the plants attacked your column.

"We understand the pressure your unit was facing and that you had little or no understanding as to what was coming at you. Frankly Captain I find it hard to believe any of you came out of that mess alive.

"The base was under heavy attack and it had been infiltrated by roots from the tree line outside the base. About three hours into the battle the ground in the base literally exploded with activity and they came out of the ground all at once and attacked everyone at the same time. Captain it was a massacre.

"It was during this battle a number of personnel made a break for the Ragdelog base. That base had been set up with barriers and a dome so it could withstand any assault from the outside. As best as we can tell, about four hundred personnel made it to the base and are currently holding out there.

"This leaves you and your unit. Our advice to you is to stay put if that is possible. We have determined the rocky areas are a problem for the plants and they cannot function in those locations. So, as long as you stay in the area of the rocks, we feel you will be relatively safe, any questions?"

I looked over at Brad and nodded my head. "Fleet we receive and are moving to areas of cover during the bombardment. In addition, we will set up a bivouac in the upper ridgeline area and stay put until further notice. Right now, we figure we can hold out for a week to a week and a half. Sir how long before you can bring us out of this area?"

There was a short pause and then the Admiral came back online. "There we have a problem Captain. It appears the plants have some form of antiaircraft weaponry. It is accurate and deadly. Any attempts we've made so far to fly in close to the ground has resulted in heavy losses. Until we can overcome that issue, we will be unable to extract you from the planet. Our advice to you is to set yourself up to live off the planet until further notice.

"Captain I'm sorry to say this but you are on your own for the foreseeable future. We will keep in touch and will attempt to make supply drops to both you and the base in the Valley. You will be notified when we will attempt a resupply. Good luck."

Well that just about said it all. It was obvious we are not going to get any help at that time. I stood there looking out across the valley and then had a thought. I turned and looked up into the mountains. From where we were standing the higher regions had no plant life at all, the entire mountain was clear of all forest, undergrowth, or other plant life. It was obvious that's where we needed to be.

I called Brad and Sergeant Dent to where I was at. We sat down and I started to lay out the situation we were in. We had twenty-one personnel and some weaponry with ammunition. One man had a severely damaged leg and the rest of our personnel in various states of shock. That was it, that was the totality of our unit and what I had to work with.

I advised Brad and Sergeant Dent we would be moving our people up into the higher regions above the base. We are to look for any caves or places we can take cover in and build fortifications for our defense.

Our next concern was to start looking for means of feeding ourselves and maintain a water supply. Sergeant Dent was assigned to take three men and start looking for water.

Brad would be looking for any means or methods in bringing about a food supply.

With that, the entire unit headed up into the mountains. We had no idea just how long we would be living in that region, all we knew was for our own safety we had to be away from the plants, as far as possible. At the same time Sergeant Dent took his three men and moved off to our southeast looking for a water supply.

As we moved back up the mountain, we started to come across more pockets of men who had made it out of the trees below and up into the highlands and rocky areas. In short order I had picked up thirty-seven additional troops. Unknown to me at the time, Sgt. Dent was picking up additional troops as he moved east across the face of the mountain. When he showed up later on, he would have an additional twenty-four troops besides his three-man search team.

It was maybe four hours later when we came across the first in a series of caves we had seen dotted across the face of the cliffs. A large number of caves can be a problem and the problems were the selection of the best cave we could defend and was safe in itself. Though we had never seen any form of animal life on the planet did not mean that there were no animals living there. In addition, we wanted a cave system that gave us ample room to move around and set up additional fortifications.

Within two hours we found the perfect cave, a cave that gave us a good commanding view of the region below us all away down to the base. Inside it was separated into five fair sized chambers. One would almost think they had been prepared just for our need.

In a place where the plants are the dominating life, what do you look for to use as fuel for a fire or, for that matter, a number of fires and that became an issue, a really big issue.

Well anyway, we had our shelter and I had good hopes that Sergeant Dent would return with a water source and we would come up with some type of fuel we can use for heat. If we were able to fulfill all those needs, we would be set as far as our living needs were concerned.

The next thing after that was dealing with our survival needs. After securing our survival needs, we will work on the means of dealing with the plant life on this planet.

Bottom line, all I wanted to do was get back to the fleet so we could leave this area and return home. I had no more desire to remain here in this place.

About two hours later Sergeant Dent returned with good news, he had a water source and it was not too far away, in fact it was just inside the next cave.

With Dent's return with the additional troops, they had found and those I had located we now had a total complement of eighty-two troopers. Not only that, we also had additional weapons and ammo that had been in short supply. Things were looking good.

The next thing was to carry out an exploration of the cave we had selected as our primary defense location. I left Brad in charge of the others and took five men and started back into the cave. Every twenty-five yards we used a laser cutter to mark the wall of the cave as a guide for when we came back. I planned on a one-hour trek into the cave before turning around and coming back.

As we moved into the cave it was not unlike most other caves I had been in before. Things didn't start to change until we were probably a quarter-mile back into the cave. I noted the walls started to show more and more quarts and other crystalline forms. By the time we had moved another quarter-mile the reflection from the walls of the caves of our lights lit the place up like you were standing out in the midday sun. And there still appeared to be no end to the cave.

At the three-quarter mile mark, I decided to stop and leave things as is and return back to the base and plan on re-exploring the cave tomorrow. It was clear there is far more to this cave complex than I had anticipated. As we turned and started to head back, I heard a sound coming from behind us further on into the cave. It sounds like a low hum like that of an electrical motor running in a room behind a closed door.

I stopped, turned, and decided we needed to go on to see if we could find that hum, it was something I could not let go of. We back-tracked ourselves and headed deeper into the cave to find whatever that hum was.

It didn't take us long, in less than an eighth of a mile further in we came to a large chamber and dead center in the chamber was what appeared to be a machine, a large machine. This I had not expected. This was completely outside of what I had thought we would find in this cave. The first question that came to me was. Is this a Ragdelog machine? The second one was. Are there any of them here in this place at this time?

We stood there looking at the machine and the room. It then dawned on me there was light here. This chamber was well lit with artificial lighting. It had come on when we entered the chamber. Clearly it was a major find and clearly it was of an intelligent creation, but who and when?

My greatest wish was that we would find an exit out onto the other side of the mountain range. Instead, I ran headlong into another mystery. Damn, this is unreal I had not expected anything like this and to top it off we now had to worry about who made it and if they were still here. One thing I knew for sure we're going to have our hands full.

Let's assume this thing was built by somebody other than the Ragdelogs and this base or whatever it is was still functional, what would that mean to us?

As I stood there looking at the machine and the room it was sitting in, I decided I wanted to know what was behind all this. So, we started back to our base to prepare for tomorrow, because I planned on moving everybody to this location at that time. As we walked out of the chamber and back to our bivouac location the lights in the chamber went out.

It was two days later and we had brought everybody to the room where the machine was sitting. We had carried out a complete search of the area and had found over a dozen rooms branching off from this main room. We found dining facilities, sleeping facilities, a hospital, office facilities, and supply and maintenance facilities. The way it looked right now we were set.

As we extended our exploration of this new facility, we were finding equipment, video security units, and computers, none of which we had any idea what they said, what they meant, or how they worked. This is going to be a major job trying to gain an understanding of how this thing functioned and what it was for.

We brought everybody into one of the meeting rooms we had located and had them set at the tables and started a brainstorm session regarding the facility. It was during this time I discovered one of our troops was a linguist. It was obvious what he was going to be doing in short order. Others that were with us had training in mechanics, cooking, and just about any organizational application we would need.

First thing we did learn was that the place was abandoned. How long it had been this way we were not sure; all we could say was whoever had been here was no longer here. In fact, we could find no trace of anything that would shed light on who had lived here and built this facility. It was a total mystery.

Further digging around in the facility, we found storage areas with large amounts of foodstuff, some of which we had no idea what the hell it was. I guess the only way you can deal with something like this is to try it and we did. Know what? Most that stuff tasted pretty darn good.

So, here we are eighty-two people sitting in the middle of a mountain in the middle of an alien facility with all the food and water we needed and absolutely no idea as to what the hell to do next. One thing we could be sure of, we were going to survive, and that was not going to be a problem. Now we had to deal with the fleet and what we're going to do in order to leave this planet.

Just at this time Brad and Sergeant Dent approached me. Brad sat down across the table from me. "Alex, I don't know what the hell we found here but I have a feeling we're just beginning to discover everything this place has to give. To be quite honest with you, it scares the crap out of me. I guess what I'm saying is that we need to put together some kind of a plan as to what we're going to do next, would you agree?"

I sat there looking at them, realizing that yeah, he was right, there had to be some action taken in order for us to move on. We had at our disposal a complete facility that was buried deep in this mountain range and totally protected from the plant life that controlled this planet. Yet there was still a lot that needed to be done to ensure our survival.

The next week flew by and in that time, we had managed to get much that needed to be done completed with the few people we had. We had managed to work our way to a point where I was able to contact the fleet. Upon hearing our situation, it was decided we would remain in this facility and form up a permanent outpost. The fleet would then return to their home base and prepare to return and carry out a total invasion of this planet.

The following day the fleet formed up and headed out and away from this star system and back to its home base fully thirty light years away. That left us here to carry on with our own survival and to try and learn as much as we could about this alien facility we had stumbled onto. We had no idea what was waiting for us.

We started to send scouting units out on a daily basis looking for more stragglers and trying to determine what the plants were doing down in the area of our base. We knew there were still people out in the old Ragdelog base trying to survive. It was our hope somewhere along the line we would be able to make contact with them and bring them out of that area.

Over the course of several days, we put together a fairly good knowledge of the activities of the plant life on that side of the mountain down where the two bases were located. We were able to formulate a plan for bringing those people out of that base and up to our facility.

"We're looking at high risk and probably a fairly large casualty rate," I told Brad. "But we had to try, and if we're successful we could use those people."

We had learned there were actually four hundred three people out in the old base. Of that number four of them were injured and still in recovery. That would mean we had three hundred ninety-nine able-bodied men to add to the eighty-two here at this base that would give us four hundred eighty-one able-bodied personnel with six in recovery.

While digging through the storage facilities of the aliens we found a number of what appeared to be weapons including explosives. One item was readily recognized as some type of flamethrower and so we brought those out of storage. We took them out into the open, outside the cave, and tried them out, they worked perfectly. That's when the plan really came to mind, we would use the flamethrowers to literally burn our way down to the base and back and probably not lose a single person.

A second weapon was located in the storage area and it turned out to be a plasma cannon. At the time we were not sure what the hell it was, but once we figured it out it would become the key to everything we did from then on. This weapon would give me the tools I needed to tear this planet apart from stem to stern. The really good thing about this weapon was that there were sixty working cannons available.

We contacted the people at the base and advised them in two day's we would start the attack. They were to put all their equipment, everything they could carry in to packs and be prepared to move out at nine hundred hours, forty-eight hours from now. They advised they'd be ready and able to move the most important of their equipment with them.

On the morning of the attack, we had forty-five of our personnel armed with flamethrowers. The remaining thirty-seven were used in four areas; Spotters for directing fire from both the flamethrowers and plasma guns, four three-man teams with plasma guns placed at equal points in the command for direct fire on the plants, and the rest divided into rifleman units for close in fire and selective fire assignments. There were the recovery teams whose job was to move in and assist the base survivors in their task of clearing out of the base.

We knew the ground was going to be our primary problem and so we had fashioned a number of items into a snowshoe like arrangement that we could wear and would give us the ability to keep from sinking into the ground and to stay on top of it and hopefully help avoid the roots.

The attack started at the base of the ridge on the first line of trees. We hit them with a full line of attack using the flamethrowers and literally tore them out of the ground it was a massacre, you had to see at the believe it. When the flamethrower hit the trees, they screamed and the blood poured out of them. When the fire hit them, it ate right through them and they went down. We then pointed the flamethrowers at the ground itself and burned it to a depth we felt would keep the roots from gaining access to us.

At the same time, we had the teams of plasma guns working the perimeters of the flamethrower attacks and cutting into the ground and opening it up so the flamethrowers could penetrate easier and make it faster for us to reach the base.

We worked our way down through the forest out into the open areas and down to the old base. To our surprise as we moved around the base down by the valley, we saw the remnants from the base out in the valley making their way towards us. We fully expected to see them hit by the creatures before they got to us but they made it. I think the plants were as surprised as we were by the effectiveness of the flamethrowers and plasma guns.

As they came into range, we opened up on both sides of them raking the ground with a flamethrower set at the highest possible level with the deepest possible penetration, again aiding this action with the plasma guns. Once we had formed up, we then moved back around the old base and headed for the ridge.

We were making good headway and had moved about three quarters of the way to the ridge where we had our first casualty. A large root had emerged from the ground off to the east of us and had managed to target one of the troops walking on that side of the formation. There was nothing we could do for him he was literally speared and pulled out of the formation and dragged underground before we could react. We never saw him again.

Even at that we are able to make the ridge and clear the area with only the one casualty. By fifteen hundred hours that afternoon we had everybody back to the new base and settled in. At that time, I checked to determine who the highest ranked officer was in the group, it turned out to be a lieutenant by the name of Bob Chisel.

Along with Bob there were five other sergeants and two corporals. This meant I was the highest ranked officer of all those present and that gave me command of the facility and the personnel.

We now had the personnel, four hundred eighty-one able bodied troops, needed to start an in-depth study and learning phase of the alien facility. Job tasks and duties were assigned and passed out and new tactical plans were developed. Everything came together like clockwork. We had a well-organized and committed unit.

Chapter Five

Ghosts from Times Past

Our first need was to try and determine who had been the originators of this place. Whoever it was had built a facility that was beyond impressive. It was still running and we had no idea as to how old it actually was. We knew there were all kinds of rooms and facilities built into the mountain. The one thing I was looking for was a control room and an administrative room or office.

It only took a short time to find the control room and shortly after that they found what appeared to be the main administrative office or command offices. With that we started to study the control systems in the main control room and I took a team to the administrative offices and we started to search that location as well.

Great care needs to be taken when searching a location where there is little or no knowledge of who built or lived and used this facility. In this case it was all a mystery. Right away we started to find what we thought was recording systems and document retention systems.

As it turned out we found no paper at all, just stacks of perfectly square pieces of metal about two inches square and maybe a quarter of an inch thick. They were all one color, pastel rose.

There had to be five hundred of the things in the cabinets behind the main desk in the office. On one side of each disk were markings that had been applied like someone had taken a pen or some other device and printed a label on the disk. What the label said was unknown, I had never seen marking like these before. One thing I did know, they were not Ragdelog.

I took several of the disks and sat down at the desk and set them out in front of me with the label up. I sat back and took a long look at the desk top. The first thing I noticed it was clean, just as if someone had come in that morning and wiped it down. There was no dust at all on the desk.

The next thing I saw was an object sitting on the far side of the desk directly in front of me. It was approximately ten inches high and about that wide. From front to back it was maybe an inch thick. It appeared to meld into the desk top and in fact was part of the desk top. To my right was an area of the desk top that appeared to be smoother and transparent although I could see nothing under or in it.

Directly in front of me was a part of the desk that appeared to be padded. That is, there was an inlay on the desk top that was soft and pliable. To the left was a ball built into the desk top that appeared to be floating in the indentation it was sitting in. Other than that, the desk top was empty.

I then pushed the chair back and looked at the face of the desk and found several drawers down both sides, there was no central drawer as most desks usually had. As I reached down toward one of the drawers my hand came to within six inches of the drawer and it automatically slid open. As it opened, I drew my hand away until the drawer reached its stop.

Inside was a treasure trove of items. At first glance I had no idea what they were or what they could or would be used for. What was clear was the fact that everything was neatly placed in the drawer, not a single item appeared to be out of place.

I then placed my hand back in front of the drawer and pushed it forward and the drawer withdrew from my hand and into the closed position. I then moved my hand down and opened the next drawer and the same thing happened. I did this with each of the three drawers on both sides of the desk.

It was when I got to the last drawer on the left side, I discovered something I recognized. As the drawer came open the only item in that drawer was a gun. I sat there looking at it, trying to come to a realization as to just what it was, I was looking at. Yes, it was a gun, but this gun was something I had seen before, in fact this gun was worth its weight in gold.

It was an old gun from a time in my world's history that was well known to most every military trained member of our armed forces. At one time this weapon had been standard issue to the officers of the United State of America Army. This gun came from a time that was six hundred years in our past Yet there it sat in absolutely perfect condition. Next to it were three clips for the ammunition it used.

It was absolutely beautiful. The gun was a Colt .45, 1911 combat automatic weapon. I sat there looking at the thing and shaking my head. I couldn't believe what I was looking at. What the hell anyway. This thing was so out of place all I could do is sit there and shake my head.

I finally reached into the drawer and picked it up and brought it up closer to my face so I could get a better look at it. Brad, who had been looking over a number of items over by the door to the office, saw me pull the gun out and up to my face. He walked over and looked at the gun. "What the hell?"

I looked up at him. "Yeah, it's a Colt alright and a perfect one at that."

"How the hell could that be?"

All I could do was to shrug my shoulders. "Brad, I have no idea what to say. I can assure you that this is a genuine Colt .45, 1911 automatic and it's in perfect condition."

Brad had bent down close to the weapon for a better look. "Alex, that gun is over six hundred years old. They stopped issuing those things even before that time and changed over to the Beretta. What you have there is a collector's gun and its one that could be worth more than all your combined pay for your entire career."

"Yeah, I think you're right on that one. I've only seen one of these things and that was at the military academy and they had it in a display case. It had been owned by some general in the past by the name of Paton."

I then reached down and took the holster and placed the gun into it, after loading one of the clips, and took the other two clips out of the drawer and slid them into their receiver cases attached to the holster. I stood up and undid my utility belt and slid the holster onto my belt and fastened it back up. I then looked at Brad, "Finders keepers."

That still left the prime question that both of us had not vocalized but were clearly thinking. Where the hell did that gun come from anyway? There had to have been some form of contact between the Earth and the beings who were running this place. And of course, just who the hell were they anyway?

It was then I noted a small slot in the edge of the desk top, dead center to the sitting position of the desk's occupant. I bent over and took a close look at it and then reached out and picked up one of the rose-colored cards and tried to slide it into the slot. It would not go. I looked at it and noted the two edges had slots or grooves cut into them, one centered on the edge and the other off centered. I oriented the disk to the slot and pushed it in.

There was nothing and so I started to try and figure out how I was going to get the disk back out of the slot when the object on the desk lit up. I was watching it and sitting down at the same time. Brad moved around the desk to my side and bent over to see what was happening.

The first thing that happened was a string of some kind of writing moving across the viewer from left to right. I didn't pay that much attention to it in that I couldn't read it anyway. That lasted maybe forty-five seconds and then a picture appeared. It was of the inside of the chamber with the machine in the center of it.

Next thing that happened was a figure moved into the view of the camera and turned facing the camera and started to talk. It was a language I had never heard before. With that I concentrated on the individual doing the talking. It was a man not unlike any of us. In fact, I would say he was clearly earth originated just by the overall appearance and the way he moved.

It wasn't long before several people were looking at the viewer and trying to come up with a good answer as to who the subject was. Finally, one of the guys stood up. "Hell, we know that language. Captain, can you pull that disk back out of the slot?"

I looked at him. "I should be able to, I just need to figure the release process to get it to eject."

I looked at the slot and ran my hand over it and the disk popped out. The person that said he knew the language asked me. "Now flip the disk over and then rotate it one hundred eighty degrees and then slide it back into the slot."

I did just that and then sat and waited. Shortly the viewer lit up again and this time the same language appeared moving across the screen right to left and it was English. "What the hell, it's English?'

The troop leaned over the desk. "That's right I recognized the language he was talking in and it was English in reverse. So, the disk must have been in backwards."

That simply floored me. This was a recording of someone from a time past who was from Earth. The next questions were obvious, when and who? In just a matter of minutes everything had changed and we were now looking at a mystery that in many respects literally outweighed the issue of survival on this planet.

Someone from Earth had been here before and they were here long enough to have built this base inside this mountain. The next issue that dawned on me was this part of the base or was there more. There were several caves in this area of the mountain and when you took a close look at them their entrances were all the same or very similar.

I then called for everyone to gather in the main chamber for a meeting. Twenty minutes later all were present and we then presented our finding. Everyone was more than a little excited once they learned that the base had been held by an English-speaking race, probably of Earth origin.

I immediately set up six five-men teams to go to the other caves nearby and check them out. If the cave entrance was truly similar or the same then there had to be something inside those caves that was related to what we had found so far. Brad took command of the six teams and they headed out.

Next, I took a lieutenant and one sergeant and a corporal and assigned them as a team to review all the disks we had found, to get everything they could in chronological order so we could all go through them and find out what we had stumbled on to. Everyone else returned to their search and discovery activities.

A team had found all types of provisions in a storage area within the first cave and had been busy working up a meal for us that afternoon. The thing that was so amazing about this whole thing was the fact the place was so pristine and still operating just as if there was going to be people returning to the facility in a short time. It was an eerie effect and one that kept everyone on edge.

Yet, no matter what we worked on everything came back to who had been the creators of this place and where they came from. That was going to be interesting. Right now, we would have to wait for the team that was researching those who left this place to come up with some information. But while the team was continuing their work on that project the rest of us would continue the search of the facility.

It was later that evening when Brad and I were walking through the main chamber, when he said. "Captain, I am beginning to realize all of this is familiar in some strange way. I mean as I walk through this place and observe the overall design and makeup of the facility, I came to see it matches most any military base I have been on. Not only that, it has the same feeling. Know what I mean?"

I was looking up at the ceiling of the chamber as he said that and then reached down and felt the .45 holster on my belt. "Yeah, I think I do. This place is almost like the recruitment base I entered when I first came into the service. I had that feeling the moment we walked into this place. The problem is how could that be?"

We had stopped and were standing there looking around. "Captain that .45 you found must be at least five hundred to seven hundred years old. Those weapons have not been issued to the service for easily that long and maybe longer, yet it looks almost new."

"That my friend has me worried the most." I was starting to think there was something so outlandish going on here we needed to take precautions in how we work through this place. "I think maybe we need to back off a little and take each and every step a little slower than we have been. With that I want everyone to stand down from the searching until the analysis team has finished its examination of the disks and can give us an idea as to what is going on here."

"Yeah, maybe that would be best. I'll have everyone stand down in the morning. They could use the rest anyway. They all seem to be a little on edge right now and some time out would help."

That night I sat up most of the night looking at the .45 and wandering as to how it got to the far off reaches of the Starfield United System. Here we were in the year 2743 and I have sitting here in front of me a weapon that had not been issued since somewhere around 2000 or so. That would make it more like seven hundred years old, not four hundred. Yet the thing is pristine, it has no marks or use damage on it at all. Deep down inside I was beginning to think we would have been better off out in the open fighting the plants.

I must have fallen asleep sometime around three that morning when my wrist alarm went off telling me it was time to get up. I sat back and listened to the rest of the troops waking and starting to move around. It was odd but I noted they went about their business going into the shower facilities and taking their showers and the usual preparations first thing in the morning. It dawned on me that it was all so normal.

By eight hundred hours the mess team had the morning meal on the tables and people were coming in and sitting down to eat. Again, it appeared so odd. Just then Brad walked into the mess room and saw me and walked over and sat down. He was looking around at the rest of the troops and then back to me.

We sat there in silence for a moment and then he leaned forward and across the table to me. "Captain this place has me concerned. Have you noticed the normalcy of the troops this morning? I mean they're going about their lives as if this place had been their base of operations for some time, know what I mean?"

The same feeling had come over Brad and I then knew something was going on, something we needed to find out about and do it as soon as possible. "Brad I want the analysis team to push their report up. I want to hear from them by noon. If they can't finish by then they can give us what they have and then continue working the issue after that. Also, I want that briefing done to staff only, understand?"

He was watching three men sitting at the table next to us and then pointed out. "Captain these men have no idea as to what is going on here and I have a feeling they have no idea as to what is sitting outside this facility. Something strange has happened here in the last twenty-four hours and I don't think I like it."

We finished our meal and I returned to the administrative office and sat down to wait for the analysis team to report to me about their findings. Until then I was going to sit there and view some more of the disks that were in the desk and see if I could get a better handle on this place and its purpose.

107

The first disk was the normal administrative activities you would find at any base across the system, lots of data, then a few moments of personal concerns about the facility and its operation. I wasn't until disk five that things started to get interesting. This report dealt with the reported activities of a patrol that had gone out that morning. It was that patrol that had the first contact with the plants of this planet.

I sat there and read the account of the actions of the involved unit and the reactions of the commander who was making the report. It was spine chilling. "Eight hours, Fire Patrol Unit Three set out on a search and seek patrol toward the tree line at the base of the mountain. The patrol consisted of eight men, a lieutenant, a sergeant, and six troops.

"Their assignment was to work the tree line and determine if there were any native beings within the area of the base. We had been in this base now for three months and have had no indication of native life forms of any kind. That seemed strange in that the makeup of the planet would be conducive to biological activity.

"The team had been on patrol about an hour and had reached the tree line and turned and started to work its way parallel to the tree line. Weather conditions were optimal and the terrain was smooth and easy to maneuver through. The first sign of a problem was a rustling of the undergrowth inside the tree line. The team went on alert and they expected to see some animals or possibly intelligent life forms emerging from the forest. They remained on alert, waiting.

"It was maybe two minutes after they first heard the rustling that it then quieted down and all fell silent again. The team leader's orders were to stay out of the tree line but to move parallel to it and observe anything coming from that area. He ordered the team to resume its patrol parallel to the trees and had moved maybe another fifty feet when an object came out of the tree line hitting the last man.

"A root had shot up and out of the tree line piercing the man in the back and then drug him off into the forest and death. The team moved up the mountain away from the tree line and reported what had happened to the base. They were then ordered back to the base for debriefing."

I took that disk out of the reader and started another one, the next in the stack of disks. This was the report of a team who had gone in the opposite direction through the maze of tunnels in the cave system they had set up in. The report started at a point where they came to an exit from the tunnel.

The team leader reported they found a rather large opening out of the cave system on the far side of the mountain. As they approached the mouth of the cave, they could see a vast plain spread out before them. To the right they viewed a tree line and a large forested area beyond that. To the left the plain stretched out beyond their view from the mouth of the cave.

From their vantage point the plain appeared to be fairly level and covered with a tall grass of some kind. Off in the distance they could see a line of what appeared to be smoke rising up into the sky. There were five of them spaced across the landscape about fifteen to sixteen miles out. By the layout of the smoke, they were fairly sure some form of inhabitant was present. There were no signs of aggressive plant life anywhere.

The team returned to the main base without venturing outside the cave system.

I removed that disk and picked the next one up. This disk started a little different. It was a personal statement by the person using the taping system. "We will be heading down to meet with the Yallils again this morning. After yesterday's contact I felt we may have a good chance of setting up a relationship with these beings. They seem a little suspicious, but who wouldn't be when meeting creatures they have never seen before."

The Yallils, that was new and it was something that we would need to address in the not too distance future. I sat back and started to think. Here was an exploratory team of some nature who had set up a base of operation on this planet and had discovered a native species. That was almost four hundred years ago and here their base is still operational and there was no sign of the beings who ran this base.

Better still, the beings who had been here were probably from Earth in that their language was English and they were using technology that dated back some five to seven hundred years ago on Earth. The problem was we were not sure Earth had sent explorers this far into the galaxy at that time and if they did it must have been a tight secret.

Now these people have met a native culture of this planet and were in the process of bringing about some kind of a relationship with them.

I looked through the disks in the stack. There were about thirty of them. I took the last one and put it into the playback slot. "Today we leave this base and move out into the Yallils domain. We have learned that they are a friendly and generous being and have welcomed us completely to their communities.

"At this point we have developed a working communications system with them and that is improving each day. Based on our current standards I would say these beings are probably around six to seven hundred years behind us in their development. They have just entered their industrial period and appear to be progressing well. I think that we stand a good chance of becoming most influential within their social system.

"This will be the last disk I will record for some time. When and if I can return here to this base, I will provide an update to our activities with the Yallils. It is my hope our mutual relationship will assist us in returning home. Up until six months ago that appeared to be impossible. Now it appears to be probable."

I sat back and pondered what I had just listened to. It sounded as if they had been stranded here and they were planning on the Yallils to assist them in leaving this place. I must assume they were referring to this planet and hoping to return to Earth sometime in the future.

It was time for the meeting with the analysis team and so I went over to the meeting room and found everyone there waiting. As I sat down, I nodded to the team leader to start the meeting.

Lieutenant Chisel stood and took a stack of papers and moved to the head of the table. "Gentlemen, four days ago Captain Alexander directed my team and I to carry out an analysis of the data disks we found here in this facility, I will present our findings to you at this time.

Chapter Six

Rediscovering the Past

Lieutenant Chisel finished organizing his papers and the area around him. He appeared to be rather nervous and was trying to determine how he should start the show. "Almost three to four hundred years ago a contingency of space explorers landed on this planet. Their mission was that of colonization and advanced exploration of this solar system."

Lieutenant Chisel let that settle in for a second and then continued. "Though the information we have found so far gives us reason to believe these beings to be from our own planet Earth, we are not sure an assumption like that is in fact true. As a matter of fact, we believe these beings were from another place in space and may well have been a duplicate planet and society to that of Earth. It is also possible they came from another universe, a parallel universe."

Needless to say, the first words out of Lieutenant Chisel got every one's attention. I guess you could call it an attention getter. Anyway, we were now primed and ready to hear the whole story as he and his team had been able to glean out of all the information that was available to them.

He continued. "As we ran through the data disks, we found a number of issues that brought us to this conclusion. We were comfortable with the idea this base was an Earth exploration base until we started to take a close look at what it was, we were seeing. I mean, there were telltale issues that started to stand out for us and as they came together, we became more convinced that in fact these were alien beings and not of Earth.

"For example, the actual data disks and readers we were using were not in line or comparable to any of our own technology in that field. Yes, we use data disks, but the design and material are not the same? The readers were clearly unique and frankly rather intriguing. Again, their technology did not match out current or past technology.

"Next we looked at the language itself and found a number of words that were clearly alien to us. We tried to take into consideration cultural slang and word usage and none of it matched.

"No, these were words we could find no history on in our language. Our alphabet has a total of twenty-six base letters in it. We did a search of total alphabet usage in this language and found two of our letters missing and three other unknown letters included. Their alphabet has twenty-seven letters in it.

"Just with those issues researched and double checked we were able to come to the conclusion they were actually alien to us. The odds that we would run into another culture that was almost an identical culture to us has to be astronomical. Whatever the odds are, that is exactly what we have done. Are there any questions at this point?"

Questions, hell my head was exploding with questions, my problem was I didn't know where to start. As I looked around at the others, I could see each of them was trying to deal with what had been dropped on us so far.

Finally, Brad raised his hand and then turned to me. "Captain I just had a thought and it's going to be a doozy."

Brad has this way of getting your attention with his eyes and right now they were dish size and targeting me dead center. "What is it Brad?"

He adjusted himself and then started. "Lieutenant Chisel, so far, has done one hell of a job. As he was making his presentation about the possibility of these beings coming from another parallel universe, struck a chord with me.

"Captain you may remember while we were traveling to this area from our main base on Mars. We were halfway to this system when we ran head long into a space storm. Now during that time, I was working with the fleet navigation team and we had a blackout of our instrumentation. For about half an hour the fleet was without any means of determining its location and direction of travel. Normally that is not a big deal except during this time we were in the midst of a real nasty storm.

"Once we cleared the storm it took us about three hours to re-determine our position and direction of travel. The problem was at the time we detected an anomaly we could not account for. It was reported to the fleet commander and he determined it was not a major issue and in time the anomaly would work itself out of the system. It had happened before and it had worked out alright in the end."

I raised my hand to stop him for a moment. "Brad how did the navigation team take that determination?"

Brad sat back and thought for a moment. "Frankly they didn't like it. They felt it was much more significant than the Admiral had given it, and they thought it needed to be researched in detail. It was finally determined they would follow-up on it at the end of their shifts."

"Did that happen?"

"Yeah, Alex, it did and the results were scary as hell. The problem was I got called away from the team at that time and returned to our unit for preparation for our landing at the Ragdelog base."

By this time, I was interested and I was starting to have that gut feeling I hate to have when things are about to go bad for us. "Brad, did you ever hear anything else about the anomaly?"

"Captain it was the day before we landed, I happened to run into the leader of the navigation team that was on duty that night. I asked him and he almost ran off. I actually had to grab him and hold him there to get him to talk to me. All he would tell me was the fleet had made an unplanned jump and they had worked it out. He then pulled away from me and left."

I needed to have Brad continue. "All right let's hear the rest of it and take your time and give it to us in detail."

He cleared his throat and continued. "Captain, as I listened to Lieutenant Chisel it dawned on me maybe we were the dimension jumpers and not those who had been on this base. Everything matches up now even down to the plant life here on this planet. In the past, any records we had on this system indicated there was life on these planets but that they were biological and not vegetation. Captain, we had sent expeditions into this region in the past and there had been no problems with plants or any other life form here. Captain, when we jumped, we jumped dimensions and ended up here."

The place was dead quiet. I was stunned by what Brad had just said.

119

Lieutenant Chisel was nervously moving his papers around on the table top and everyone else was just starting off into space. He was right and I knew it. The problem was it meant we were stranded here on this planet for life.

I knew then and there our fleet would never be back. If they had not figured it out then they would be returning to an alien Earth and only God knows what that will result in. No, they would never be coming back, at least not to this planet in this dimension.

I let everyone have the time to deal with the shock of what had just been revealed to us. I knew I needed to get things moving again if for no other reason than to give the men a chance to shift from the shock to the process of survival.

Finally, I stood up and walked around the table and to the door of the room. I stood there a few seconds and then turned back to the men around the table. "Alright, we're stuck here, but that does not mean everything has come to an end. We still have our lives and we are on a planet that appears to be capable of supporting life as we know it. We have a strong base here and we can still function.

"With that I am planning on reaching out beyond this place and scouting the land out to the east of us and finding out just what is out there for us to survive with. Also, if there are beings out there, then they will be beings who have had past experience with those of our kind due to the past occupation of this base. Does anyone see any problem with my train of thought?"

No one responded.

I continued. "Good, now we need to expand our activities in the area of this base. Starting tomorrow I want teams to hit every cave on this ridge and carry out an in-depth exploration of those caves. I have little doubt they are caves that were built by the prior occupants of this base and we need to know what is in them and what we can use of those items, those supplies.

"Brad you and Lieutenant Chisel will work up the operational plans for the exploration of the other caves by tomorrow morning. I want all those caves entered and surveyed by days end."

Brad was busy writing down the orders and then looked up at me and nodded his head. "How many men to a team do you recommend Captain?"

"Set them up as Squad Fire Teams and make sure they understand they are there to explore not to destroy."

Next, I turned to Sergeant Dent. "Sgt., I want you to get three men and have them fully outfitted and ready to move out with me at eight hundred hours tomorrow. You and I are going to venture out onto that plains area and do some scouting of our own."

That got everyone's attention and I then turned to the rest of the men. "We need to know what is out there and we need that information right now. Our best information is that the prior force who occupied this base left going out across that plains area. My question is whether they made it anywhere or were lost in the process.

"In addition, I know by the data disks in the administrative office they had made contact with a society they called Yallils and were leaving the base to form up with or join up with that society. There is nothing on them after that notation. They left this base and went east to meet up with the Yallils and that is the last information that exists on the people from this base."

Brad leaned toward me. "Captain isn't that a little dangerous for our top command to put himself in such a hazardous situation?"

Just like a good back up man I thought. "Brad everyone needs to get involved in this process. There is no room for anyone sitting around and waiting for everyone else to take the risks and suffer the hazards of these days. No, I need to be at the head of the V where I belong. No one else can fill that position."

He nodded his head again as did Lt. Chisel and the meeting came to an end.

Everyone got up and headed out to carry out their assigned task while Sgt. Dent and I remained behind to plan for the coming scouting trip into the plains tomorrow. I looked at the Sergeant. "Well, what do you think, have I gotten myself in deep enough?"

The Sergeant smiled. "I think you're crazy as hell, but someone has to go so why not us."

With that, we started to work picking the three men we would be taking with us. We needed a radio man, a large weapons man and a navigator. Once the three men were picked the Sergeant headed out to find them and bring them into a meeting so he could get them briefed and readied for the next day's duty.

Meanwhile, I went back to the administrative office and started to look at more of the data disks that were in the desk. After about an hour I found the disks I wanted to see and I started to review them in detail. It was obvious the prior commander had taken the same course I was planning. His account of the action was graphic and disheartening as well.

I slid the disk into the reader and settled back to see what the past commander of this base had to say about their coming actions. The disk label said "Recon-in-force." I pushed the button to start the reader. "nine hundred hours and we were moving out of the compound and onto the flats heading east from the compound entrance. I had a complement of thirty troops move out and across the flats in force.

"To my left and right I had sent out re-con units to scout out the land and try to give us any advanced warning if any plant life was in the area or heading for us. Our experience on the other side of the ridge had been most difficult and we were not inclined to go the same direction. This was our only option and it had to work out for us.

"We had gone maybe three miles when the left re-con unit signaled us to stop. A runner came back and reported they had found what looked like a body of a person. It had been there for some time, but it was still clothed and had a number of items with it.

"I signaled the command to position itself in a strong defense tactical formation and then returned with the runner to the scene of the find.

"The re-con leader was still looking the body over when I came running up. He looked up. 'Chief, it is human, but not of any clan I recognize. The clothes are fairly primitive, but the items it was carrying were well advanced and on par with our own equipment.'

"I squatted down beside the re-con leader and looked the body over. We determined it was humanoid and while checking it out in detail we found an issue with its sex. To our surprise the body had the sex organs of both a male and a female, something none of us had ever seen before. The squad leader looked at me. 'Captain they're asexual or hermaphrodites.'

"That in itself was more than I had anticipated, but as we looked this body over, we could tell its build was that of a rather large man, actually a really large man. Taking into consideration the level of decomposition and shrinkage, this being had to have been around seven feet tall and weighed in at around three hundred pounds. Clearly, this was a most formidable being from our perspective.

"We tried to determine a cause of death and when we turned the body over, we found a gaping hole in its back. This being had died a rather catastrophic way. It must have been fast. We then gathered up all the equipment it had with it and then I order the re-con team to move out. I returned to my command position and we moved out as well."

I reached out and stopped the reader and sat there considering what they had discovered, an asexual or hermaphrodite being that was huge in overall size. That didn't sound good to me at the time. I restarted the reader.

"We had covered another two hours distance when we came to a mound which actually turned out to be a low ridge that ran from right to left to the direction of our march. I formed the unit into a battle line and we approached the crest of the ridge.

"The last several yards we did on our bellies. The low ridge dropped off sharply on the other side for about ten meters and then flattened out to a gradual decline. Beyond the bottom of the decline where the ground flattened out, about four hundred feet, we spotted the first structure.

"It was a simple wall running parallel to the ridge line we were laying on. From that distance it appeared to be around eight to ten feet high and maybe four or five feet thick at the top. It appeared to be made of rocks but from our distance I was not sure.

"Other than the wall there was nothing we could see in either direction or beyond the wall itself. That did not mean there was nothing there. It meant I could not see any other structures at that time.

"There had to be a purpose for this wall and it was one of two things. It was there either to keep something out or to keep something in. After our experience on the other side of the mountains I immediately became concerned we may be on the wrong side of the wall.

"Up till now we had not seen a single sign of any plant movement on the plain as we walked across it. I reasoned that if there had been plant activity the body would not be there now. No, I was relatively sure that the problem was on the other side of the wall, not this side. The question was, what was the problem? If it was plant activity then that meant some life form had built this wall was on this side of the wall just as the body was.

"The only other option was that there was life other than plant life on the other side of the wall and it was a protection from some life forms on this side of the wall. Again, not plant life because of the body we had found.

"It was clear we had to approach the wall. My problem was whether it should be in force or with a scout unit. Next, I needed to determine the route of our approach. We had to find a break in the ridge that would make a retreat easier and faster than the ridge height at our current location. Our two recon units were sent east and west to find a break in the ridge and access to the lower area and approach to the wall.

"It took them almost two hours to find the right conditions for our approach to the wall. The east unit found the route we needed and so we moved the whole of our force to that location. Our rear defensive unit had moved into position and we were organizing the advance unit when a movement further to our east caught our attention. It wasn't much, but it was enough to home in on. There was a group of unknowns moving along the wall on our east flank. At this distance it was hard to tell the number, but it was more than one. We had company."

I again stopped the reader and pulled out my notebook and made my entry concerning the found body and the observations of some other movements coming in on the force. I sat there thinking over the situation they were in and measuring as to whether the commander was making the right decisions. I felt he was. I then restarted the reader.

"My entire command dropped down and moved back except for the recon units and myself and my immediate second in command. We watched the unknowns moving toward us, staying close to the wall and moving in a single line formation. They were now within range that we could count a dozen individuals. By their movement and discipline, we knew they were military. Being on foot I reasoned their main force must not have been too far away, probably no more than five to seven clicks.

"Next I noted the individuals in the formation were not large like the body we had found. They were close to our size and appeared humanoid as well. I was concentrating on the group when our recon leader got my attention. He pointed off to our east and there coming right at us was a contingent of the biggest beings I had ever seen. They were armed and were clearly stalking the group down by the wall. We had but minutes before they would be right on top of us.

"I had little choice. In these last few seconds, I had determined the wall was there to keep these big guys out and the group below was obviously a scout unit checking the integrity of the wall. There was an ambush coming up and it would take place exactly where we're sitting, at the cut in the ridge. I made a snap decision and that was to take on the immediate danger to us and that was the big guys.

"Our entire unit was repositioned with our rear guard now working our left flank and our rear at the same time. As the giant unit came in on us, we counted fifteen of them, all well-armed and all appearing to be able to give as well as take.

"The unit below us had not noted any activity on the ridge and continued along the wall. We were set and ready to cut loose on the lead scout of the giant unit as it moved in closer to us. When the lead scout noticed us, it was too late. He turned to signal when our first rounds hit him. When the first-round hit, he reacted as if he had been stung by a bee and tried to brush it away. He then gave the alarm and all hell broke loose.

"By this time our entire firepower was concentrating on the unit of giants and we started to make our damage known. The scout went down and those behind him came right at us. I don't think they thought we were something other than part of the unit below them.

"The way they came at us, they had no respect for our capabilities. It wasn't until the full force of our fire power centered on them that they began to realize this was not what they thought it was. By then it was too late. The firefight lasted just under a minute and all the giants had gone down."

Again, I stopped the player and sat there trying to visualize the situation that commander had found himself in. Clearly, he had the element of surprise on his side and it paid off for him. Yeah, he had done exactly what I would have done. I restarted the player.

"The unit down below had dropped for cover and had remained concealed during the whole of the firefight. Once it was over, I stood up and waved at the unit below and then dropped back down and waited for their response. None came. The last we saw of them they were running back in the direction they had come from and in short order were out of sight.

"We were left with the remains of the giant unit and the understanding this was but a scout unit from a much large force. We had no alternative but to retreat back to the caves and set up a defense there. We stripped the giants of their gear and headed back to the caves double speed."

I sat there looking at the screen after it had gone black. They had walked right into a conflict region between two humanoid populations, one of which was made up of giants.

Now the question was, what happened to this base contingency? Were the giants still out there? Were the other beings still out there? And, was the wall still there? This place had been here several hundred years, actually three hundred and some years, before we came on the scene, so any number of things could have happened in that time frame.

I looked back into the drawer and found one last disk and put it into the reader. I sat there waiting for it to start when I looked back into the drawer and saw a folded-up piece of paper. I thought that was the first real piece of paper I had seen in this place that was not a part of some research file we were using while searching this base. I picked it up and opened it and found, to my surprise a hand written note in English. I started to read.

"To Whom It May Concern if you are reading this paper it means someone other than me has found and entered this facility. Good luck because you'll need it in the coming days, weeks and months. Before you view the last disk please understand we were making decisions based on the facts as we saw them. In this place, the facts never tell the real story and what you see is not and seldom will be what it appears to be.

"My best advice is to always think in your own defense and self-interests. Be greedy and trust no one. Kill first and then ask questions and never, but never accept the first answer as the truth. Be prepared to inflict pain to get to the truth. They have no concept of truth and it must be pulled out of them. They will give it, but it comes in small doses and usually in a riddle.

"Be brutal and give them no leeway of any kind. If someone professes to be a leader he or she is not, kill them outright. If they hide from you and try to avoid you, attack them straight on and give no quarter, kill until they beg for relief. These beings know no honor, no truth, no compassion, and no interest in anything other than whatever benefits their interests.

"Everything they say or do is meant to give them an advantage and if they gain it, you will die. The Deminators, those are the big ones, hate everything and anything that is not of them. Kill them on sight. The Yallils will beg with one hand and stab you with the other. You can use them, but only after you have pounded them down and they know that their actions are actions of survival and nothing more.

"Listen, this may be counter to what you have been taught and trained in, but if you expect to survive you have to be the monster, they fear the most. When you first meet them, come at them with everything you have. No holding back. You will need to wade through their blood before you can even hope to deal with them. They only learn by experience and the more deadly and terrorizing the better.

"I failed to see that and I'm now sitting here preparing for my death. My entire command has been destroyed because I trusted these beings. Realize this is an alien world and it is one that lives and survives on violence. You must be far more violent than they ever thought of or have experienced. I'm sorry, but that is the truth and that is the only way you will survive this planet.

"Now, watch the final disk and learn from it. You'll understand what I'm talking about as you watch the final hours of my life."

I sat there dumbfounded. I had never in my life read anything as unbelievable as this piece of paper, yet I knew it was right. I knew in this piece of paper was the recipe to my survival and the survival of my entire command. The question was, did I have the balls to do just as this writer had warned me to do? I then started the reader for the last disk.

"This is the third day of battle the year 2360. We have been fighting for three months now and they just keep coming. All my plans had gone up in smoke and half my command had paid the price for my actions. We had tried to make contact with the Yallils and they accepted us and treated us well because of our actions against their enemies. What I didn't know was that anything, anyone, not of the Yallils was their enemy, period. There were no alliances, no mutual interests, just enemies.

"When I finally figured that out it was too late and they had us. I knew I should have gone at them with force. That was the only thing they understood, brutal and complete force, the deadlier the better. If I had known that in the beginning my entire force of ninety-seven personnel could have had an entire million-man army of the Yallils beat and submitting to my every wish. I showed them what they perceived as a weakness and they struck. I could do nothing to change it from then on.

"We made it back to the base with forty-three personnel left and they're right behind us. We have been able to hold them off now for three days, but they keep coming, those greedy little bastards. I know now we don't have long. We have developed a plan that will keep them out of the base, but we will have to attack them head on. There is no other way. I don't want them to get at our technology and so we make this place taboo to them. They enter, they die. It's putting the fear of their god in them and believe it or not it's not that hard.

"In an hour we will charge out of here and take as many of them as we can. We should be able to make it about a mile out before they have us surrounded. The end will be rather fast by then. Their main concern will be finishing us off and defending themselves from the Deminators. I don't worry about the Deminators they are no different than these bastards and so to die by either one makes little difference.

"Listen and remember, the more brutal you are the more power you carry. Give them not an inch to move in. If you question an answer, a gesture, and look just kill them and as many as you can in the first thirty seconds.

They'll give up as soon as they can get down on their knees without dying. You can conquer the whole of this world if you have the right blood lust taking you there. Learn it now and you can survive. Fail, as we did, and they will eat you alive."

Chapter Seven

Alexander the Great

After seeing the last disk and reading the letter a second time I called Brad into the office. As he came in and sat down, I noted a worried look on his face. "What's up Brad?"

He sat there a few seconds and then leaned forward. "Captain I'm still not sure that I want you to venture out into that plain area on your own with just four other men. There is too much that can go wrong out there and right now we don't need to lose our leader.

"I've got a feeling in my gut there is something out there we don't want to meet or come in contact with. I also know that in time we must go out there and deal with whatever it is. I would prefer we do that in force and not with a small fairly vulnerable force. No, I don't think you've made a wise decision in that respect."

I sat there watching him and then handed the letter over to him. I watched him as he read the letter and then saw the change come over him. He looked at me and laid the letter back down on the desk top. "I don't know if I or you or anyone else in this command can do that?"

I nodded my head at him. "Yeah, I know what you're saying, but I also know what that other command went through and I have already determined I will, I must, so you had better get your head on straight and make the same determination.

"If we meet those beings, we will hit them hard and not stop until they are crying for relief. We will not make the same mistake the others did." I then shifted in my seat as I prepared to address the reason, I called Brad into my office. "Brad as much as I hate saying this I need to. As of right now any time we make contact with any native of this world we kill first thing. No questions, no salutes, no chances. We kill them outright and without remorse.

"I know that goes against our upbringing, but if we expect to survive in this world, we become what this world is, ruthless and deadly. We kill first, second, and third and then kill some more until whomever or whatever we are killing begs for relief. I want every man in this command to refocus their minds on that issue. We have no choice in this matter. We either live by the standards of this world or we die."

Brad sat there looking at me. He had this strange look like he was seeing someone he had never seen before. After several seconds he started to nod his head. I could see his mind working and he was preparing to say something and I needed to let him work it out.

Finally, he raised his right hand. "Alex, I know where you're coming from and I know that what you're saying is true, but I still find it hard to believe we are going to take that route. It goes against everything I have been taught and trained in. I don't know if I can do it. So, if you think I will not be able to carry out your orders I have no problem with you removing me from my command position."

That set me back and he could see it. I sat there and let what he had said roll around in my mind and then decided I needed to turn him around. I needed him and he knew it, but he was loyal enough that he was not going to become a burden for me. "Brad, don't think for a moment this is not hard on me as well. I hate the idea of what I have decided, but I also know if we plan on living on, then we have to fight for the right to survive.

"We are aliens here in this place and as a result we are not a part of the social or power system that exists on this planet. The other commander of this base found out the hard way and has left us with clear and direct information as to how we must conduct ourselves among these beings.

"No, I will not accept your removal from your command position. I trust you and have complete faith in you and I know that for the good of this command you will do what must be done. In time this command will die off simply because we have no way of maintaining our age and ability to live. That I find unacceptable. We are here in this world and it is our permanent home. We will become a part of this place. We will take control of this place and it will be as we desire it to be. If it means killing untold numbers of natives to get them under our control then that's how it will be, even if I have to conquer the entire planet."

A smile moved across Brads face and he pointed a finger at me. "You're Alexander, as a member of the Starfield United System, you were Alexander 6 and here in this place you will become Alexander the Great. For some reason I have no doubts you will achieve that position and you will rule this world.

"As small as this force of ours is, it will eventually rule every living being in this place. With a future like that coming at us, I can do nothing but submit to your desires and support you. Just remember me when you're the Great."

I stood up and reached out and took Brads hand. "I don't know if it will go that far, but I do know we must fight to survive and I can't do it without you. Forget you, no my friend I would just as soon die."

With that Brad stood there and waited for my next order. The final act of the beginning of the conquest of this planet was now starting and we had much to do and little time to do it in. A new force would come out

143

of these caves the likes of which the beings of this world had ever seen or ever experienced before, a force so violent, and so powerful that many would fall before it without lifting a hand of resistance.

The following morning Sergeant Dent, his three hand-picked troops and I left the cave and started across the plain in the same direction the prior command had gone three hundred years earlier. The only difference was this new force had a better understanding of the makeup of this world and what was needed to overcome it.

Once clear of the caves I sat the team down and went over the methods and processes we would be using if and when we made contact with any of the natives of this world. I held nothing back and gave it to them in cold and direct sentences. "You see any living being, you shoot to kill right off the bat. No hailing, no gestures of friendship, no attempt to make a peaceful contact. You will kill them on the spot to the last living creature. By that I mean if they have dogs, or horses, or camels, or any other type of animal with them, those will die as well. They will be stripped of their equipment and then left where they fell."

The team sat there nodding their heads. They knew the meaning of deadly force and were not concerned with the taking of life. They had seen enough of it on the other side of the mountains and were determined never to be in that situation again. With that I ordered the Sergeant to take the point and we set out. I was particularly interested in finding the low ridge and then seeing the wall beyond it. I had no idea if it would still be there or not, I just needed to try and locate it so I could verify what the prior command had related in his letter and disks.

Maybe three hours later we came upon the ridge, just as the prior command had described it. As we moved on to the top of the ridge, we could hear a lot of noise over the ridge. It sounded like a war was going on and so we all went on alert. As I got to the top of the ridge and peered over the edge, I saw a fairly large contingent of beings in the valley below working on the wall. The noise was the sound of hammering and building. There must have been two dozen beings there working on the wall, repairing a large gaping hole in it.

It was obvious some kind of a fight had taken place there. The hole in the wall had scorch marks all over it and the ground around that location was all torn up. Over to one side was a pile of large beings. We were seeing the aftermath of a fight between these two sides. I knew the prior commander had been right about his remarks and that set my mind that much harder on the course I had planned to take.

One of my troops reached over and tapped my shoulder and then pointed to our left or east of us. Sure enough, there they were, another unit of the giants moving down the valley, along the wall toward where the others were working on the wall. Within moments the unit doing the repairs saw the giants coming and they prepared for a battle. We watched as the two sides formed up and then all hell broke loose.

We watched the melee for maybe ten minutes as the giants were slowly taken down by the fire power of the defenders. The last of the giants fell and then the others returned to their rebuilding job. It was now our turn and I set the troops up in battle line. There were only five of us, but the fire power we were about to unleash was unmatched by anything we had seen so far. I gave the order and in less than thirty seconds the remaining force was annihilated.

You have to see a fire unit such as those in my command to understand the force and power that hit those beings. No, they didn't have a chance and that was just the way I wanted it. I wanted to send a message and in killing them the way we did; a message was clearly sent. There was someone or something new in the neighborhood and it was something to be reckoned with.

The next time I came back it would be in force, more force than any of these beings had ever been faced with. Out of the caves the gods would be sending an irresistible enemy that could not be stood against or bargained with. It was to be either complete submission or total annihilation.

We then looked for and found the break in the ridge line and went down and cleaned all the equipment we could carry from the dead. We left the area and headed back for the caves. We had left a message and in a short time it would be followed up with more. I knew then and there that I was on the right track. Power, unabridged power was the key to this world and we were going to demonstrate a power base the likes of which they have never seen or experienced. The conquest had started.

Chapter Eight

The Conquest Begins

We returned to the base and I sat down with the team and my command unit. We laid out our actions and our confirmation of the facts the prior command had left behind. We turned the weapons we had taken over to our arms officer and he set to work analyzing the makeup of the weapons and their effectiveness. That report would come back later.

Right now, we were entering into a full invasion plan for the region we had just been to. I was looking at a two week turn around and then an advance force into that region until we located and made contact with either side of the battle we had witnessed. At that time, we would start the systematic destruction of whichever society we found first.

The following day the arms officer reported his finding to my command staff and me. The weapons were not any particular threat to us. Basically, they fired a solid object that appeared to be made of metal. That object was found to be similar to the rounds used in the old .45 I had holstered to my side. Nothing indicated they had any plasma or laser weapons of any kind. Clearly, we were looking at armies that used weapons that were four to five hundred years behind ours. They were not a match and that gave us the win before we even started.

On the second day back from the scouting mission the command unit sat down and went over what had been discovered in the cave system we had occupied. What was to follow would be so far beyond our wildest anticipation that we could hardly begin to assimilate everything.

They had found a total of five excavated caves in the system. Each cave was roughly the same size as the first one we found and were living in. In each cave there was a central chamber with a power station running in the middle of that chamber. After a closer look it was determined each of the five power stations were linked together and the power, they generated supplied the needs of the five caves plus.

In the middle cave, two caves from our original one and the center cave of the five, they discovered a lower level. This level was massive and contained a manufacturing facility the size and complexity of which they had never seen before.

Within a short period of time, they came to understand this facility was capable of making or producing anything we wanted. That meant we had a weapons factory right there on base and we could produce more of what we had and new technology as we developed it.

Upon hearing that, a plan started to develop in my mind. A plan so crazy and so terror filled it scared me. It came to me I wanted to go back to the original base of the 943rd and recover the rest of our supplies and unit equipment. To do that I knew I had to clear a path to approach the base, but I wanted more. I wanted a demonstration of such firepower any being anywhere on this planet who heard about it would experience a level of fear never seen before in this world. My goal was to completely destroy the entirety of that forest and every plant on that side of the mountains, down to the last blade of grass.

It was one week later when we took two hundred of our total complement of four hundred eighty personnel and headed toward our original base. With us we were carrying a new plasma cannon that made anything we had in the past a child's toy. My plan was rather straight forward. We would start at the tree line and move down to the trail killing and burning every living plant or creature between us and the base. It would be a total and complete annihilation of every life form on that mountain side and across the plain below us.

We moved into the area and set up the cannons. I could see the plants turning and watching our every move. Clearly, they were ready for a rematch, but this time it was going to be a completely different kind of rematch. We were there for blood and a lot of it. In the end there would be no life left in that region or valley. We were going to sterilize it of all life forms, total and complete destruction.

151

At high noon the first cannon started firing on our right and as it moved down into the main growth the second, then third and then every other cannon on the line joined in. It was a melee of activity in the tree line as the plants were cut down and burned. The first cannon reached the trail line and then moved back up to the starting point and then fired into the ground penetrating to a depth of four feet.

The ground just rolled with activity as the guns stripped the life out of the ground. Once we reached the trail line along the whole of our front, we moved the cannon down for the second assault. The same story held true in that assault and we cleared the ground of any living plant life down to the flats and start of the plains area.

A strike force moved in along our left flank and entered our ground base looking for any survivors. None were found and we then prepared for our attack on the old Ragdelog base and the search for any more of our people. By this time the larger plants out on the plain had started to move into the area of the base. We had reset our cannon and started the attack for a third time.

As the first of the plasma cannons hit the plains, the ground exploded with plant activity. The ground was literally full of root systems and we laid down a barrage of such magnitude that nothing could survive it.

We had stripped the ground of life out to the old base and then moved out across the plains area with our strike force and entered the base. Much to our surprise and pleasure we found thirty more of our people holed up there.

We collected more of our equipment and then took the newly found personnel and headed back for the caves. We kept a continued barrage of plasma fire going as we moved back up the mountain to the caves.

I planned on sending a scout team out the next day to see if the attack results were total or if we would need to return again and hit the area for a second day. From what I had seen so far, our first day through had done the job.

This gave me the pleasure of knowing that we would not have to return to the area ever again. We had demonstrated the firing effect of these plasma guns was exceptional and they would clearly work well for us in the weeks and months ahead.

After we made it back to the caves, I met with the lead officer of the contingent of men we had rescued from the old Ragdelog base. His name was Sergeant Davis. He related to me the methods they had used to fend off the plants while holed up at the base.

They had secured an area that consisted of a concrete basement and walls. Their main concerns were the doors and windows and those they covered with steel plates that were bolted in place. Their problem was the need for supplies and he advised they were nearly out and would have needed to leave their safe zone shortly to try and find additional supplies.

They were literally within hours of having to make that move and they were sure none would have survived. The plants had made it a habit of coming to the doors and windows of their base and making an attempt to break in or do it just to let them know that they were still out there waiting for them.

That morning they had heard the noise of the attack up on the mountain side but had not attempted to leave their bunker and reach out to us as we came to rescue them. It wasn't until the guns were turned on the plains area, they realized someone was coming for them.

They spent the rest of their time there preparing to leave and taking everything, they could carry.

When the rescue troops came knocking on their doors, they were fearful of opening up, but once everyone started talking back and forth, he had his men cut the doors open and they came out. It was the greatest feeling they had ever had. Now they wanted to know what had taken place during their time locked away.

I went over the full effect of the first encounter with the plants and the level of casualties the 943rd had taken. Once that had sunk in, I went over the situation with the fleet and the fact we had actually made a dimension jump and when the fleet left, they were heading back to a main base that was not their base but the base in this new universe. We felt we would never see the fleet again.

With that we then went into our activities on the other side of the mountain and our plans to move into those areas taking on the native forces we had discovered so far. The sergeant seemed to be more than a little into our plans. He was carrying a hell of a lot of hate in him and he was looking for anything to vent that anger.

Once the briefing was complete, we then assigned the sergeant and his team to positions within the overall organization of our current unit. We had a total complement of personnel now numbering five hundred ten.

We also had a range of weaponry between the systems we brought with us and the ones we had found here that had been left by the prior command. That is where the plasma guns came from and the other weapons gave us an advantage that would prove to be overwhelming to those we would be facing in a few short days and weeks.

Two days later we were ready to initiate our second scouting foray into the new area. This time we took three hundred of our people and left the remainder to cover the base. We had installed automatic plasma guns in the mouth of each cave entrance. Those remaining behind were to ensure nothing came within a quarter mile of any cave entrance no matter what or who they looked like. No one or nothing was to approach the caves unless it was me in person. If we failed to return, they would know that fairly soon. So, their orders were firm, I or a member of my command unit had to approach the cave entrance and none other.

We headed out in the morning on a scouting mission in force. We were prepared to take on anything we came across. You may call this a scouting mission, but if we come across any other forces, we would be taking them on and giving no quarters. This was the start of a reign of terror that was going to sweep across the face of this world and leave the native population in total and complete disarray.

As we walked across the plain toward the location of our first contact, I found myself thinking about what had taken place over the past week and how I came to this state of mind where I was willing to kill anyone or everyone in order to control our environment. I had to admit the change started to set in as I listened to and read the letter from the prior commander.

I had no idea what really became of those people. He, the commander, had clearly returned to the base and left the letter and the data disk for someone else to find. Nothing else followed and I had no idea if he or any of his command survived, I doubted that any of them did. I knew they had left the cave system and attacked the natives head on in a death or suicide attack. All I could do was speculate about the end results to their lives. I made a mental note to keep a watch out for any signs that would point out what had happened to the prior command.

We had a good idea as to what they had looked like through the data disks and all the pictures that had been incorporated into those files. Something told me I would see signs of their markers in the natives of this place. I hoped that there would be stories of the battles and death of the aliens who had invaded their world.

It wasn't long before the leading point of my command reached the low ridge and its view of the old wall in the valley below. Any signs of the last visit we made here had been erased. The wall was rebuilt and all bodies had been eliminated. You would think nothing had taken place in the area of the wall in the last hundred years.

Because we had noted that anytime we encountered any of the natives they were always coming from the east, our left. So, I directed our lead unit to turn east and stay up on the ridge. A rear guard was set up to follow behind by ten minutes keeping a watch for any action coming in from any direction on us.

It wasn't long before we started to see signs of activity around us. The rear guard reported the first of the activity on the other side of the wall. A force of unknown numbers was moving parallel to us on the other side of the wall with four spotters walking the top of the wall watching our main force. I felt a sense of satisfaction settle into me as I received the information from the rear guard.

They were doing just as I had determined they would do and we were now working our way into their trap. I passed word we were within a mile of an attack on us and we would be prepared to take a direct attack from our front, our left side and left rear. A section of my command to my right dropped down to the flats next to the ridge we were moving on and then dropped back and set up as a counter attack when the enemy force was fully engaged with us. They would also blunt any attack from the wall to our right.

It came to my mind just how the hell did I know that would be their plan of attack? Why did I feel so positive I knew what they would do and when and where they would do it? I was beginning to realize I knew more about this place and what was to come than I should have. As I puzzled over that feeling

159

and realization, I felt the time of our first encounter come on us.

As I looked ahead, I realized we were at our destination and we would be fighting in just a short time. How the hell did I know that? I ordered my right flank to anchor in position and had the left flank started to move out into a battle line and then brought their far-left flank to make a ninety-degree wing at that end of the line.

The counter attack formation was set and in position and the rear guard had set up as a blocking position in the event of any rear-guard attack. I knew these people were not that sophisticated and would attack head on and hope by sheer numbers they would overcome us.

I had to keep an eye out for the giants. They just seem to show up wherever any group of any size of the other natives was around. I then realized I needed to improve the designations for these two groups and so I settled on giants and normal. The word was passed to all units so they could respond appropriately when the word came.

So, we were set and ready. It wasn't ten minutes before the first attack started. They came at us over the wall and spread out on our right flank coming up the rise approaching the ridge. At this point the access to the ridge was fairly easy and the ridge was much lower than the areas behind us.

When the Normal's were three quarters of the way across the flat area between the ridges and wall, my right flank moved into firing position and set to repel the attack. I sent a word that there were to be no survivors in the attacking force. All were to be killed to the man. The acknowledgments came in from my unit commanders.

As the attack reached the base of the ridges the right flank shifted into fire position and brought their weapons to bear on the attackers. I gave the command to fire and the entire line lit up like a thousand suns. The sheet of fire hit the attacking line and completely engulfed it and brought it to a dead stop. As they piled up below us their attack started to break up. We had them cold and they knew it.

I could see the first indications of a retreat starting to form up and I gave the command to shift target and half our line shifted its fire to a point behind the attacking force. As they tried to retreat, they ran right into the line of fire and we then carried out the annihilation of the complete attacking force. Not one made it out of the field of our fire. To the last being we killed them all.

I looked across at the wall and saw the one I knew was the commander of their forces standing there watching the destruction of his entire force I walked up onto the ridge and looked across at him and then he turned and dropped down and out of sight behind the wall. I then sent units down to check out the bodies and make sure everyone was dead. None were to be left alive.

As the check of the bodies was carried out, we reformed our lines and checked for any dead or wounded. We had one man with a slight cut on his forehead. No major issues were found and everyone was in a state of heightened excitement. Once the body count was completed, we reformed and continued moving east.

We were coming up on our night bivouac location and needed to find a location that gave us optimum coverage and field of fire in the event of a night time attack or early morning attack. We found a great location and set the camp up with plasma guns ringing our site and set for automatic activations. They would go off selectively and take out anything that came within the safety zone of the camp, whether animal or man.

Once settled in I had my command team meet in my tent. We laid out the coming day's activities. We completed an in-depth review of our actions that day and then set to looking over the next day's plans. We would continue east searching out any other forces of any size and eliminating them.

We knew somewhere out there were one or two major population centers, one for the normal and one for the giants. We were hoping to find one of them before heading back to our base and then taking that center out in total. The complete destruction of a major population center would cause more terror among the populations of this world than taking out a single armed unit in combat.

The night was uneventful and at six hundred hours the troops were up and preparing their meals. By eight hundred hours we were on the move again going east. I had sent a quick strike unit out ahead of us to attempt to locate our next target. They weren't gone twenty minutes when they called back and reported they had found the main center of the giants. It appeared to be well fortified and defended. The unit was ordered to remain concealed and the main force would be there in less than thirty minutes.

As we came into the area of the fortification, we could see the structure from a good click out. It appeared to be about four to five miles in diameter and had several buildings in the inner city that were well over ten stories high. The walls around the city were probably twenty feet high. Other than that, we could not see too much going on in the city.

Up until now we had seen no forms of transportation other than on foot. I assumed the reason for that was they were not that technologically advanced and there were no ride-able animals or live stock on this planet or this immediate area of the planet. That was about to change and it would also change our ability to move our troops and attack any future enemies we may encounter.

We were fully in position around the city when we saw the first indication of mechanical transportation in the city. It was an odd-looking contraption that was cruising along the top of the wall. From our position it appeared to be floating along above the wall and it was carrying one giant on it in the prone position. He was on his belly and appeared to be steering with his hands on a double control stick setup.

I brought my binoculars in close on him and could see he was positioned on the machine much like someone would be while riding a motorcycle back home except this was completely prone, giving the machine a very low profile. If we had one of these, we could carry two men on a single machine.

It was maybe forty minutes after our main force reached the city, we heard the alarm go off inside the city. In less than ten minutes when the first salvo came at us from the walls. No one was hit and everyone stayed in place waiting. Over the course of the next hour the city defenders had fired salvos from three different weapon types. That gave us the information we needed on the level of resistance we would be meeting.

They had no idea as to our size and if they knew we were only three hundred total troops, they would have come at us in force. That would come, but only when I was ready for them. We finally finished setting up our weapons and putting everyone in position when I gave the order to show ourselves to the defenders. We had no sooner showed than the wall lookouts had determined our force was minor compared to their overall strength.

In less than fifteen minutes the gates to the city opened and a large contingency of giant troops came out the gate. Half were on the transporters and the other half walking. I gave the order to take out the transporters first knowing full well they would use them as a shock force to try and break us up and cause a panic. What they didn't know was they didn't have enough troops to cause any level of concern. This was going to be a massacre, followed by the complete destruction of the city itself.

Once in formation their command gave the attack order and the transporters sprung forward coming straight at us. I was impressed with the speed of the devices and moved my response order up by thirty seconds. The signal was given and a sheet of fire shot out of the defensive line and hit the line of transporters head on. It was devastating. Not a single one got through and that left the foot troops of the giants faced with having to deal with us. They stood there looking at one another and their command not really knowing what to do or whether they wanted to continue in the assault.

We never gave them a chance we hit them with our plasma guns and laid the whole of the force flat in ten seconds time. I then ordered the guns on the gate and the wall and we turned them up to full force.

Meanwhile I had split my forces and sent two units of fifty shock troops to our left and right circling the city and taking up positions to cover the back of the city. Sure, enough the gates opened and a line of giants started streaming out of the city. The troops let them get about a hundred yards out from the gate when they cut loose on the line starting at the gate and moving out from the city. No one survived.

We now had them bottled up and they were going nowhere. I knew one thing I could not allow them to surrender. This had to be total destruction. We had no means of dealing with beings this size. To let them come close in and within our troops was inviting real trouble. No, the giants had to go and their future had been decided.

We set up to destroy the city and all within it. The plasma cannons were moved into place and at twelve hundred hours the assault began. At first it appeared nothing was happening until we saw a cloud of dust start to come out of the rocks that made up the wall around the city. Within minutes they started to crumble and that was followed by a total collapse of the wall.

With the wall down the buildings within the city started to come apart and in a short time they too started to collapse. After about an hour of continuous plasma fire the city laid in a dust pile with no survivors. We cut the plasma guns at that time and then sat there waiting to see if there was any movement from within the city. There was none.

I ordered four scout units into the area around the city to look for and eliminate any survivors, again there were none. We did find several of their transporters outside the walled area and took them for future study and development. We could use these machines for quick response actions.

That night we bivouacked outside the walls of the destroyed city and would be heading back to our cave base in the morning. The men needed a rest and we needed to go over all we had learned so far about the beings of this world and then plan our next assault.

The night was uneventful and we headed out for our base the next morning. We used the same scout and cover formation we had been using. As we approached the turn north heading for the cave base, we noticed considerable activity at the wall below the ridge we were moving along. These beings were like ants, always working on the wall and putting everything they have into it. The pile of casualties we had left as we came through that area the days before was gone and the damage to the wall was nearly repaired.

They saw us coming and moved within the wall and then set up a defense system in the event we may attack them. I stood there looking down on them knowing they were reacting like any group of people who were terrified of what they had experienced so far. We were a clear threat to them and they were not likely to throw themselves at us like they had that day.

No, I could clearly see their methods had changed and I would need to take that into account. It didn't matter, they were next on my list and there was nothing they could do about it.

That evening we arrived back at the base to find it was damaged from an obvious attack. One of the plasma guns had been knocked out and there were a number of pieces of hardware lying around outside the defense perimeter of the base. As I approached the main cave entrance the lieutenant came out to meet me.

I looked around. "How many dead or injured?"

"No deaths, but we had one bad injury. Not sure if he will survive at this point."

I looked at him and could see he was a little shook up over the situation. "All right let's go inside and sit down and you can go over what took place here."

We went into my office and the rest of my unit went to work cleaning the place up and clearing the area outside the base of any objects or debris.

The lieutenant sat down at the main conference table with me and my command team. I looked at the man. "Lieutenant Miller, would you please fill us in on what took place here? Please be detailed and don't hold anything back."

"Sir, we had no problems the first three days you were gone." He was referring to his notes and paused and then continued. "On the fourth day, yesterday, we noted they had scouts working out beyond the base. They were moving up and down the full width of the cave complex. It was obvious they were checking for ways and means of attacking us.

"I put the base on alert and we then set up waiting for them. I did not venture outside the base itself but chose to wait until they came at us. It was about noon when they hit us. I would estimate they had a force of three to four thousand troops coming in on us and I opened up as soon as they were within range.

"We tore them apart as they came in. They had been using a wheeled contraption to try and shield themselves from our plasma guns but it did them little good. The remains of those shields are still out there. We took more than half their numbers in the first hour and after that they started a hit and run game with us. That was when they got the hit on our plasma gun and wounded my troop.

"By night fall they had pulled back and we could see them moving off and away from us at that time. The next morning, today, they were all gone and we stayed put until you came into sight."

I sat there looking at him and nodding my head. He had done a good job based on what he had told us. "Did you get videos of the attack?"

He smiled and reached over and laid a data disk in front of me. "Yeah, we got great shots of the entire attack and pull out. It will give us good intel on how these beings fight and what their current plans are."

"Miller, based on what you have said and what I've seen so far you did one hell of a job here. You go back to your men and pull them out of service and everyone is to take the rest of the day and evening and relax, you earned it." I was satisfied with his work and the way they had carried out their duties.

As he got up to leave, I took the data disk and put it into the reader and let it run. It was just as he had reported, except for what we saw within the line of the attacker. I looked over at Brad. "Did you see it?"

He was sitting there smiling. "Yeah, couldn't miss it. They are a little primitive in their methods, but they told me everything I need to know about their method of fight."

I popped the disk out and then turned to the staff. "All right, I want this disk duplicated and each of you to take a copy. I want you to spend the next two days studying this disk and the methods and process this attack force used while they were here. Get it all down on paper and ready for a planning session day after tomorrow."

They all got a copy and then left and headed out to carry out their assignments. I got up and walked over to the maintenance cave where the transporters from the giant's city had been taken. By the time I got there they had one of the machines stripped down and lying-in parts all over the repair bay they were working in. As I walked up the maintenance sergeant walked over to me. "Well, what do you think?"

"Captain, these are rather interesting devices. Their technology is surprisingly advanced and with a little added effort they could have made flyers out of these things." He was picking up a section of cable while talking to me.

"They have a levitation system here capable of considerable speed and range. With just a little more effort they could have been airborne and fully capable of carrying weaponry."

I looked at the pile of metal and cables lying there on the floor. "What will it take to

173

duplicate these devices and even move them into the flying stage?"

"Captain, I can take the three units you brought back and bring them back into full operational capabilities. In addition, I can give them more speed and higher elevation. As far as actual flying with the ability to maneuver and carry weapons I will need to build short wings for carrying the weapons and to increase the maneuvering characteristics of the craft." He was walking along the line taking a hard look at all the hardware there in front of us.

He then turned to me. "Captain, I can have a fully operational craft in a week. Now as far as building more of these things, that will take a little longer. However, after looking the supply storage facilities over in this base I believe I have most of what I need right here. Give me a couple of days to research it all out and I'll be able to give you a clean time line."

That was good enough for me. "Good, get to work on it and when you have everything worked up come and get me and we'll see what we have."

To date we have had three major encounters with the beings of this world and have come out of them on top. With only two casualties to show for all the fighting we've been in I would say we're looking good. What was needed now was a major move against these beings who had attacked our base and we had to beat them bad, bad enough for them to submit to our rule and control. This was going to be interesting.

Chapter Nine

The Taking of a City

Over the course of the next two days, I was able to move around the five caves and get a good look at and build a good understanding as to what the prior occupants had left for us. In each location I noted my troops were in high morale and well rested. I would have a fully fresh force when we returned to the field and our next contact with the forces of this world.

The Giants (Deminators) had been severely impacted by the assault on that one city. By now the other Giants cities will have determined the status of the city we had destroyed and hopefully had gone there and witnessed the destruction.

The Normals (Yallils) had lost a considerable sized force when attacking our base and had also seen a smaller force destroyed by our field force. They would be deeply concerned about what was coming at them.

In addition, during our viewing of the battle at the base Brad and I had seen something none of the others had noted while the Normals forces were retreating. I now knew where the prior command had gone and knew they had lived for some time with the Normals.

Within the command of the Normals were a number of beings that were different from the rest. Their stature and overall appearance were clearly like ours and were probably fathered by the prior force's personnel at that time.

If that were true then the Normals had accepted them into their social structure, but had not given them full citizenship. In time they had probably gleaned everything they could from the visitors and then turned on them. For that they would pay as well. A change was coming to this world and those living here would either go along with it or would be left behind, dead.

On the second day everyone assembled in the meeting hall and we started going over what we had learned from the videos of the Normals assault on the base. They had good discipline until one crucial event took place.

They, the Normals, were coming in on their third assault when they were able to take out the plasma gun in the center cave's mouth. With that the other gun zeroed in on their leading edge and the first casualty they had was their leader.

He went down and that changed everything. The assault ended and the Normals started a panicked retreat, taking their dead and wounded with them. They folded with the death of their leader and there was the key to every battle. Their leader and his death changed everything.

They had no means of backup for a fallen leader. He was everything and no one was prepared to fill his place at the moment of his death. We made a note of that and I knew this social system was based on power. That is, those who lead gain their position by building the greatest power base and holding it.

That meant when making decisions the leader made them all and he allowed no one else to carry any leadership capability. In that way they had only one head and when their head fell their unity and ability to fight went as well. Not only did we have the fire power to beat them, we had the strategy we needed to beat them. We identify and then target the leader.

The next thing I noted was when one became leader, he had to demonstrate he was the leader in everything and anyplace. So, when it came to battle the leader had to be up front or out front in order for him to maintain his control and position of power. That placed him right in our sights.

I thought back to the meeting at the wall with the unit of Normals we wiped out and remembered the leader standing on the wall. The mistake I made was I did not target him. In the future I would not make that mistake again.

We were ready and finished our battle plan for the next day. We were going to go after the Normals this time and it would probably mean the breaching of the wall and then taking them on in their own territory. The key to the whole plan was the wall breach and that needed to be done quickly and the size of the breach had to be significant. It had to be a breach the likes of which they had never seen before.

The next day the troops formed up. We took the same size command, three hundred troops, and loaded up the plasma cannons onto the new transporters. We also loaded up with additional ammo and supplies. As we left the base the remaining defender unit set the plasma cannons on auto and zeroed them in at the predetermined range and then left them that way. We had built shields for each cannon and then doubled each one up at each position. Anything of any force that came against them will never get within two hundred yards of the caves.

We followed the same route back toward the wall. We had gone out maybe an hour and a half when this feeling came over me. I pulled Brad aside and stood there looking out over the prairie to the east of us. The ground cover, or grass, in that area was about twenty-four inches high and I found myself concentrating on the grass. "Brad, move the cannon on this side up to this point and fake a break down and bring those guns to bear on the grass out in that direction. I will keep the line moving until you're ready to fire and then call for a combat drop.

"I'll set it up so the rest of the guns on this side are ready to go in to action when the first one opens up."

Brad was still a little confused by my actions and I then leaned in close to him. "Brad, that tall grass if full of Normals and we've walked right into a trap and they are almost ready to spring it. We have maybe five minutes before they hit us, I want to hit them first."

Brad's eyes lit up and he nodded and moved over and started to work. In less than a minute he had brought the transporter to a halt and started looking it over. They also swiveled the cannon out toward the grass and I moved down the line and set the other cannons on alert.

I looked up toward Brad and he nodded and I gave the command. "Hit the ground." And everyone dropped in unison. At that moment the first cannon went off and started raking the grass. Almost immediately they came up out of the grass and then the rest of the cannon came on line and we literally cut them down. Some broke and tried to run, but we were on them in seconds and brought them down.

Just then the right side of our line started shooting and I turned and sure as hell they had a second force on that side. Our people had been on top of everything and they cut that side down just as fast. When things finally calmed down, we had suffered one casualty and had wiped the entire attacking force out.

I immediately pulled my strike unit sergeant aside and ordered him to go into the field and make sure every last one of the enemies was in fact dead. If they were able to locate and identify the commanding officer of the force and he was still alive I wanted him brought to me. I had the rest of my command stand down and ready to repel any other attacks that might come.

The strike unit found twenty enemies alive and dispatched them in quick order. There was no commander found in the field. They finished their sweep and moved back to our lines. I passed the word to Brad to move out and be prepared for more action as we approached the wall. They knew we were there and they were going to fight us all the way. That was fine with me and it gave me that much more incentive to kill everything and anything that was not of my command.

Our scout units were starting to see more activity ahead of us. As we approached the ridge above the wall the level of activity was like an ant's nest. They knew about the ambush and their entire force had been destroyed, that was obvious. Now they had the wall itself fortified and ready for a frontal attack.

That may have been the way the Giants or Deminators did it, but they were about to learn a frontal attack was not the way we did it. It was just beautiful; they had tied themselves down to a static defensive position and that gave me the ability to cut them to pieces. They were about to learn a lesson of a life time, but it would be one that they would never be able to take advantage of.

Their defensive line extended to my left and right with a total area of about a quarter of a mile long. I would estimate they had five to six thousand people on the line. They outnumbered us by at least twenty to one. From an attacking forces perspective those were impossible odds to go against. But we had several things in our favor.

First, it was the land. The low ridge we have become so familiar with is still twice as high at the highest point of their wall. We would be shooting down on them.

Second, they had selected a static defensive strategy which gave to me all the maneuverability I wanted. I could move my forces, no matter what the size, and control the actual progress of the battle to my advantage.

Third, just by sheer size alone the defenders would have a difficult time communicating along their lines. My line of communications was a fraction of theirs. This gave me more fluidity and theirs tied them down.

Forth, was for the fire power; with my plasma cannon I could completely overcome the wall and anything on it or behind it without sacrificing a single troop. In the process I would be decimating their line. Their casualty rate would be huge compared to our forces.

No, this was going to be a lesson in the ability of a smaller attacking force being able to overcome and destroy the larger defending force. I still had two things I needed to know. The first being the identification and location of their commanding officer and his command staff, I wanted that commander alive and before me. He would be used at the right time and place as another visual lesson for these beings.

The second was the position of the sun when we start the attack. Right now, their sun was almost directly overhead. I wanted it down to our backs when we start. That will put them looking right into it and give us a clear line of sight for our targeting needs.

It was perfect. We had the time we needed to move the cannons into position and while doing that keeping our people low and out of their line of sight. When the time came, we would only have to elevate the cannons and depress the barrels for a direct attack on the wall.

We positioned the cannons along the ridge to our left and right so we had a complete coverage of the wall and the personnel behind it. We made sure our cannons were spaced out between the extreme left and right guns so that we could rake the wall its entire length where their troops were positioned. We would be able to take down a good third of a mile of wall before we were done.

We settled in and waited for the sun to get into position. The troops needed the rest and time to have a good meal and get all the water they would need over the next few hours. In addition, our scout units were busy making sure our rear area was clear of any unknowns. I had little doubt they had put all their plans into defense of the wall.

When you think about it that has been their focal point all along, that wall is the most important thing for them. It's their survival, their security, their life. In a few short hours that life would come to an end.

Things never seem to turn out just as you had planned them. Our scout unit called in and reported an enemy force coming from the west on our west flank. It was about three quarters of a mile out, but was moving fast and coming directly at our flank.

I immediately swung one of the right flank guns into position to take that force out and then alerted the left flank to be ready for action from their east. Further observations determined the force coming in from the west was more of a harassment force and not a full-blown attack force. I then got word of the same type of force coming in on the east or left flank. We were ready for them.

I decided to let the harassing force come on in and stage their attack on us. I would meet them head on and then when they were under control, I would launch the full attack on the wall and the forces behind it. We had maybe twenty minutes before all hell was going to break loose. Everyone was ready and keyed up. We were going to take on a force that could easily have destroyed us if they had applied their personnel properly. They didn't and were now going to pay for it.

The left and right flank forces hit us at exactly the same time. It was a well-coordinated attack but we were ready for them. At first, we took them on with small arms fire and let them work their way in to close proximity with us. It was then the plasma cannon engaged both forces at almost exactly the same time. We knocked them down faster than they could think.

The action lasted maybe ten minutes. When we were finished, we were able to take about a dozen captives total from both sides of their attack. Included in that dozen was the commander of the left flank attack. I had the captive marched into our lines to the center of our lines and then up onto the ridge so that the opposing forces could clearly see them.

I had them stand there facing the wall and then cut the entire dozen down and let their bodies drop off the ridge and to the ground below. Before their bodies hit the ground below the order was given for all guns to fire and we hit the wall with every gun we had.

The power of these plasma guns is absolutely mind boggling. If the prior command of the cave complex had used these weapons when he had the chance the outcome of their situation would have been entirely different. We had learned from their misfortune and were now taking full advantage of that which we had learned.

As the first blasts from the guns hit the wall it seemed to withstand the hits and then it started to shudder. I would say from the time of the first gun hit to the start of the shudder was just seconds. At that point the wall started to fail and then moved into cataclysmic failure. Once the wall collapsed the guns kept on firing into the area behind the wall right in on the unprotected troops there.

I got word from the left flank the troops were trying to surrender, but I order the fire to increase. Right now, they just wanted to quit, I needed them to beg, to throw themselves on their faces and literally melt at the thought of this attack continuing.

It wasn't five minutes later when we saw that happen. They poured out of the wall area throwing their selves to the ground and burying their faces in the dirt. Finally, the last of them came over what remained of the wall and went prone on the ground. I made them stay that way for several minutes before sending troops in to pull them together and ensure they were unarmed.

As our troops moved in from the left and right, one of their troops jumped up and started to shoot at the approaching victors. I ordered the gun at that point to rake the ranks of the prone troops killing about two dozen including the lone aggressor.

Lesson to be taught, failure to do as you're told is death not only for the fool who failed to follow orders, but for his fellow troops on either side of the fool. It was clear the lesson sank in deep and quickly.

The battle had lasted maybe ten minutes. At the time they finally gave up I would estimate maybe eight hundred gave up and including their commander. As we moved in and took their weapons and checked the other side of the wall for hold outs, they identified the commander and brought him to me. It was at this point it came to me.

In old history, back in our time or dimension, when a victor accepted the surrender of an opposing force, he, the victor, would take that opposing force leader and cage him and then take him to wherever they would be going as their location of control or their main governing locations.

Here in this place, I had no such place, but they had a major location where their people lived and carried out most of their societal activities. I was going to take this commander to that location.

Our first problem was what to do with those who had surrendered. We also had a communications problem with them as well. As their commander was walking up to me, I heard one of his people yell something. The surprising thing was it sounded like the person was yelling "Help us."

I looked at Brad and he shrugged his shoulders. "Captain, that sounded like English to me, I don't know how, but it sure as hell was English."

I was a little set back by it and then decided to pursue it. "Brad, bring that man over here. Let's see what we have here."

As their commander walked up to me the man who had yelled out for help was dragged over to us. I looked at their leader, a tall man with a strong face and hard eyes. I then looked at the trooper and could see the fear and helplessness in his eyes. "Do you speak as I do?"

He stood there looking at me and then nodded his head. "Yes, we speak the same."

"What is your name?"

He didn't respond at first but stood there looking at me and then at my men as they worked in moving his troops into more controllable positions. "I am Cochran." He replied. "Why are you here killing my people and destroying my wall?"

I smiled. "Why are you trying to kill us in the first place?"

Evidently, he didn't think it was funny. He straightened himself up and then said in a demanding voice. "You will give yourselves up to me and my command and you will be taken to our leaders and judged and then executed. Do you understand?"

I continued to smile and slowly pulled my .45 out of its holster and pointed it at the trooper who had called on this man to help him and pulled the trigger. The round hit the

191

man dead center in the chest and he went down like a rag doll. I then put the gun back in my holster. "Do you have any other statements or questions to ask?"

His face was ashen and his eyes were on fire. "Why did you do that? You had no reason to do that?"

I again smiled at him. "You gave me the wrong answer and each and every time you do that, I will shoot another one of your troops. If need be, I will kill every single one of them and then take you and go find your city and destroy it down to the last living being and then I will kill you."

The look in his eyes went from anger to absolute fear in just about the time it would take one to draw a breath. He lowered his head. "What do you want of me?"

"Good for you, now we can get something done. Where is your main city from here?"

I had beaten him and he knew it and was now looking for another way around me.

He looked off to the east and then raised his arm and pointed in that direction. "The city is that way about ten miles from here."

"Good, now, how many of your people live in this city or place of yours?"

He again looked off in that direction. "We are a city of sixty thousand."

I could see his mind working trying to come up with some means of getting out of this situation. I knew then and there the commander of the base had left all the data disks had been right on the money about these beings. They were deceitful and always looking for a way to get on top of you. My reactions would have to be so brutal only terror would register on his mind.

I turned to Brad. "Listen, we're in a tight situation here. This guy is going to do anything and everything he can to screw us over and we need to kill that right here and now. Take a hundred of his troops over there to the wall and kill them. Be prepared to do it to the next hundred and so on until I tell you to stop."

I could tell he was having a hard time. "Captain, are you sure we want to do this? I mean these are our prisoners now and we need to consider that."

I took him aside. "Brad look at me. We have no choice. These beings are going to kill us the first opportunity they have. Our only defense is a superior fighting force and pure unadulterated terror. I don't like it either, but it's what has to be and you know that."

He was nodding his head again and then turned and headed toward his team. He looked back and smiled. "I think we're about to rip this butt heads brains out."

I turned and looked at the commander and could see he was paying close attention to what we were doing and saying. "What are you wanting of us?"

I looked him straight in the eyes. "I want your complete and absolute allegiance to me and my command. I want your people to commit themselves to me and only me and to follow my directions and order to the letter. However, I don't think that is possible for you and therefore there is only one way to handle this situation and that is what we are going to do now."

Just then Brad's unit opened up on the hundred troops they had taken to the wall. The commander started to scream at me. "What are you doing? That is animal, you can't do that."

"And just what am I supposed to do. If you had or were to get the opportunity to capture us you would have done this same thing and had done it much sooner."

He hung his head and then turned and faced the remained of his troops and yelled. "We are all going to die so get up and fight."

My first round went through the back of his head and he went down. The troops lay there watching and then buried their faces in the ground and started wailing. I knew then and there I owned them and needed to start the processing of them right then and there.

Their commander's body was hauled away and thrown on top of the others and then we started pulling the remaining troops out fifty at a time and taking them aside and laying out their obligations to us. In the end we gained another four hundred troops. Brad was standing there watching them clean up the battle field. "Captain how the hell can we trust them?"

I nodded at him and then turned to the new troops under my control. "Brad the one big difference between these people and us is they live a life of absolute domination. Someone is dominating them all the time and they cannot function unless that is true. I now dominate them and they will do as I tell them and do it now or face death. They know I will kill anyone of them the second I think they are not under my control. That is how they live and that is all they know."

He stood there looking across the ground at the defeated troops sitting there. He started to nod his head in understanding. "Yeah, you're probably right on that. So how are we to treat them?"

I felt myself smile, he was seeing the big picture now and I laid it out for him. "Look, treat them as you do our own regular troops. Be firm and expect them to react as you order and to do so without question.

In the beginning you will have to be hard on them and that may mean you may have to put one or two down in order to drive the situation deep into their minds. But once they see the picture and understand their situation they will comply.

"It is important you treat them the same as our regulars. That gives them a choice, either the old ways in which their lives were hell or the new way where they are treated as men, as individuals. Got me?"

Brad smiled back. "That makes all the sense in the world. All right, we'll do it that way and see what happens. You really think we may have to dump one or two before things really firm up?"

"Brad, I think we will have to. We'll cross that bridge when we come to it. Just be prepared to do it and to do it on the spur of the moment. Don't come back to me for permission. If the situation is tight and you need to make a point then do it and then let me know."

I was now looking the conscripts straight on and they could hear everything I said and knew full well what I was saying and what I meant.

We had turned the corner on these beings and they knew what their situation was. They would do as told and would die doing it. I couldn't help feeling somewhat sorry for them at that point, but I knew they would turn on us the moment we let them think they had a choice.

No, terror was the only thing their social order understood and terror was the one thing we needed to use to its ultimate end. In time they would gain a greater allegiance to me, but right now they were in that twilight zone and needed to work their way through it. It would come. They would come to understand they were in a far better situation

197

under me than they ever had been with their own.

We had taken on a major action in the past day and a half and were triumphant in each of the two major actions so far. Now the biggest of them all was before us and with an army of over seven hundred I had all the muscle I needed to achieve what I was reaching for. The next move would be the first large city of these beings and its defeat and control.

Chapter Ten

Taming of a People

We moved onto the other side of the wall and the lead scout team with one of the new conscripts moved out ahead of us working its way toward the city. We had learned we were eight miles from the city and it was walled as well. The total population of the city was said to be around forty-seven thousand, the prior commander had lied about that. Our new troops had advised there were considerable amounts of armament within the city and they would not hesitate to use them.

A mile out we could finally see the city. As a comparison I thought of my own home town and could see this city was not that much unlike my home town. There were no large or tall structures. It did not appear there was anything over three stories, that I could tell from my vantage point.

We could already hear the sirens going inside the walls as we came to a stop about three quarters of a mile out. My command team gathered around me and we took a good look at our new conscripts. They appeared to be a little nervous and I knew these guys would lean with the winning side as would their allegiance.

One of the leading troops walked over to us. He asked to be heard and I recognized him. "Sir, I don't know if our people can attack their own city. We all have family and friends in there and it's most difficult for us to even think of attacking. Sir, would it be possible for us to stay here and wait till the town falls and then go in and assist in bringing them under your control?"

I was watching him and knew full well this little creep was playing both sides. They're just that way. This was going to be a critical point in our relationship with these people. I had less than four hundred conscripts there with us. I was faced with a hostile city and a highly volatile group of troops. The situation called for the most direct and hard-hitting reaction on my part.

I looked at the man who had asked to be heard and then over at the group of men he had walked away from. I waved that group, there were three of them, over to us and asked if that was how they felt. I watched closely and finally saw what I wanted to see. The man who had come to me and asked the question was not the leader. It was the older man with the other three. I pointed at that man and waved him over to me.

He walked up and I could see the control he had and the attitude he carried in his eyes. "So, you don't want to attack your city?"

He looked at me and then turned and looked at the others and then the first man that had approached me. "Sir, were you talking to me?"

He had the innocent look on his face and I then leaned toward him. "Yes, sir I am talking to you, you could not walk over here and ask that question yourself on the off chance I may react to the question in a violent way. Is that right?"

He shrugged his shoulders. "Sir I'm not sure what you're talking about?"

His English was a little strained, but I had learned fast to listen to the edge in their voice and not so much what they were actually saying.

I reached out and put my arm around his shoulders and started to walk him back and away from the other three of his kind. "Trooper I am saying you had your friend there come to me and ask me about your troops attacking the city and the fact you have family and friends there. I don't have a problem with the question and understand the concern in the hearts and minds of your troops.

My problem is you lacked the courage and respect to come to me yourself and ask that question. You instead sacrificed your friend in the event I may reacted violently to the request. That sir is my problem."

He stopped and turned toward me. The look in his eyes told me he had figured it out, what I was referring to that is. His mind was going full speed at this time and his feet were digging into the ground. He was getting ready to act and he had only two ways to go. Either to run or attack me, he chose me.

I caught his right arm mid swing and drove it down to his side with my left arm and then planted my right elbow into the middle of his chest. That put him down. I then drew my .45 and put one round right between his eyes. I turned and walked back to the remaining three troops and went right up to them. The fear level in their eyes was over the top. As I walked up to them, I holstered the .45.

They all seemed to relax somewhat. I then pointed back at the man on the ground. "He died because he was dishonest and had placed his fellow trooper here in danger. I understand your concern for your fellow citizen in that city and because this trooper had the courage to come to me and voice that concern, I will not require you or your fellow soldiers to take part in the attack on your city.

"Second, when we attack it will be to take the city in as whole a condition as we can and with as few civilian casualties as is possible. Do you understand?"

The three of them stood there. You could see the bewilderment in their eyes and then the realization that they're concerns were being addressed in a fair and understanding manner. All three nodded and thanked me.

"Now return to your troops and advise them I want them to separate in to teams of fifty men each and to move out to the perimeter of my forces and sit down and wait for me to call on you. Is that understood?"

They all nodded and ran off and in a much shorter time span than I had expected my orders were carried out to the letter. Brad walked over to me. "That one .45 round did more to bring those people under you than all the talking in the world."

I turned with Brad and watched the troops moving out of the way and into their assigned positions. "Yeah, they want to be treated fairly and right and once they saw that, it made all the difference in the world. All right now, let's get to work on taking this city."

With that my troops set to work preparing to take the city. I had a plan that would protect the civilian part of the city while taking the resistance out of it. Instead of hitting the walls at the top I wanted to hit them low, down at the base so they would fall either straight down or out and away from the city.

We started the attack two hours later and concentrated our fire power on the base of the walls. It took a little more effort but finally the walls started to show the impact of the plasma cannons. When it finally started to move things went fast. As the walls dropped, the resistance within the city cranked up their fire power, that is until we hit them full force with the plasma cannon. It was one hour and thirty-nine minutes from the start of the attack when the flags went down.

We held fire and I sent for the three troops I had dealt with earlier. When they walked up to me, I pointed at the city. "You will go into the city and contact the command of their military unit and advise them they are to surrender now. All troops are to exit the city with all weapons and pile them one hundred yards out from the remains of the wall. I then want the military commander here in front of me. Is that understood?"

The same man nodded his head and assured me it would be as I demanded. I looked at him. "You understand what will happen if my orders are not carried out to the letter?"

"Sir I place my life in your hands if we fail to fulfill even one letter of your command."

"All right then. Go and bring them out."

The three of them took off running toward the city as the lead trooper took off his shirt and started waving it over his head. They disappeared into the city and we sat and waited. Brad asked. "How long you going to give them?"

I sat there looking at the smoke curling up from the walls. "I don't know. I'll have to face that when it comes. I have a feeling it won't be long, but we'll have to wait and see."

The first hour went by fairly fast and as we approached the hour and a half mark, I saw a man climbing down over the broken wall. It was my trooper I had sent in to contact their command. He came running across the field from the wall and up to me. He stopped catching his breath. "The city commander will surrender but there are conditions."

I stood there looking at the trooper, watching his movements. He was nervous as hell and having a hard time controlling himself. "What is it? What are you holding back?"

He looked at me and then back at the city. "Sir they have my wife and kids and have told me they all die if I don't get you to come into the city. They plan on killing you the minute you walk through the gate. I know my telling you this will probably get my family killed, but then I want to go in and kill that commander myself, in person."

He was now mad and I reached out and put my hand on his shoulder. "Your family will not die. You will stay here and let me handle this, all right?"

"Yes sir, whatever you command sir."

I looked him straight in the eyes. "Whatever comes of this you have earned yourself a strong position in this army of mine. Do you understand?"

As I said that he smiled and nodded his head. "Yes, sir I do. Sir my name is JuJu."

"All right now, let's go get that family of yours out of there safely and teach this commander a lesson or two on truth and justice."

I turned the trooper and with my arm on his shoulder walked out in front of my army and with a loud speaker addressed the city occupants.

What I was about to say could well mean the difference between our being successful or a complete and utter failure. "Commander of the city I stand before you at this time to give you the opportunity to surrender with grace, respect and honor. You have but thirty minutes to comply with my demands. At that time, I will level this city and kill every single resident of the city. Anyone who leaves now and walks out to our lines will live, those who stay behind will die."

I let that sink in for a few seconds and then continued. "Commander of the city you will release the family of this man standing beside me, his wife and children and parents and in-laws. They are to come out of the city first unharmed and uninjured. If they do not then every person trying to come out of your city will be killed on the spot. The decision is yours. If I have to start killing, I will not stop until every rock in the city is covered in your blood."

That must have hit a nerve in someone because it wasn't five minutes before the trooper beside me pointed his finger at a woman and children and several others coming over the wall. "That's my family." He turned to me and dropped to one knee and took my hand and kissed it. "My commander, I give my life to you to use me as you desire."

I pulled him up. "You're a good man. Go, meet your family."

He turned and ran off meeting and holding his wife and children and then turning and walking them back to our lines and through them to the back where they all sat down. Ten minutes later the rest of the military forces from the city came out with their weapons and stacked them up and then moved over to the designated area and sat down.

Last to come out was the commander. I walked out to meet him. He was a stern looking man so full of pride it was leaking out of every pore in his body. He was dressed like a king and everyone around him was subdued and totally controlled by him.

I pointed at several of the people with him and directed them to move off to the side. At first, they refused. They actually didn't know what to do. He finally waved them away from him and then stood there looking at me. "You think you have beaten us?"

"I can assure you that you have not. In time we will wear you down and then kill you, all of you. We did it in the past and we'll do it again." He still had that arrogant expression on his face.

I turned half way toward my lines and then the people sitting off to the side. I had positioned myself so my .45 was out of his sight. When I straightened back around, I had the .45 in my hand and leveled on his guts. His face went white and he stood there. "You can only resist as long as you're alive."

Before he could speak, I hit him with three rounds right though his guts. The people who had been standing and walking around him jumped about a foot off the ground. Seeing their lord and master dealt with in that manner literally shocked their senses to the core.

As the commander dropped to his knees, he looked up at me and started to say something but nothing came out. I then raised the .45 and pulled the trigger again and sent a round right through his forehead ending his threat to us.

I turned to his entourage and walked over to them. I was watching for the tell tail signs of someone in authority and there he was sitting in the middle of the group looking right at me. I pointed the .45 at him and waved him up and over to me. As he walked up to me, I started to walk around him looking at him from top to bottom. "It's one thing to be a leader and commander of people. It's entirely another thing to send one of those who follow you out to be killed in your place. That is the sign of a power leader and a coward."

His mouth was dropping open with every word. "I don't understand what you're saying to me?"

I was looking him right in the eyes. "You understand much too well what I am talking about."

I then spit on the ground in front of him and continued. "You are the type of being who will use anyone and everyone for your own survival. The problem with you beings is you're too arrogant to really understand what is going on here. You get yourself in a position you didn't earn and you force others to do things you would never do yourself. You're the lowest form of being and one who deserves nothing but contempt.

"You sent that man in your place and he carried out your orders even when it meant his death or the death of others. He knew if he did well, he would find himself in a position where he would gain over all the others from your city. He was playing a power game and for that, he died."

211

I stood there looking at this being and could see the first signs of fear start to crawl across his eyes.

I then turned back to the rest of those sitting there, those who had been around this man. "I should have the lot of you killed for hiding this being or trying to. That tells me you are not here for honorable reasons."

At that point one of the women raised her hand. "Sir we have no choice in that matter. If we do not do as he tells us he will have our families executed. We do as we are told to keep them alive. If I die for that and my family lives then so be it, but my family will live."

I looked at her and knew she was being honest. I then turned and called out "JuJu."

Seconds later he was standing before me. "Yes sir."

I smiled at him. "JuJu these beings here have been under that monster's control for long enough. Would you please, see that they all get back to their families and their families are all well."

JuJu smiled at me. "That my Captain I will do with joy in my heart. They will be well taken care of, just as you have directed."

With that he turned to all of them and took them off to be reunited with their families. I then turned back to the commander from the city. "You have demonstrated a total lack of concern and care for the welfare of those under your control and protection. For that, you will die, but it will not be honorable."

I then turned to Brad. "Take him over to that gate there and hang him."

Brad smiled. "Justice prevails. Damn you're good at this."

The commander from the city was crying by this time and begging for relief as he was drug off to the gate. His command sat there watching as he was tied, the noose put around his neck, and pulled up off the ground and tied off. As they tied the rope off the citizens and troops from the city all stood and started to clap their hands. They continued to clap until the commander stopped moving and then to the person they turned and bowed their heads to me. The city was mine.

With that, I had JuJu and the other two men who had been with him brought to me. "JuJu I want you to take over the cleaning up of that wall and moving the people back into their homes. Now listen to me. No one will take advantage of any body's situation. Do you understand that?"

He was looking right in my eyes. "Sir you mean we cannot charge money for our services or take items that are not ours?"

I smiled at his simplistic way of putting things but he hit it right on the head. "That is right. From now on you are serving our city not taking from it. For your services you will be paid a respectable wage so your family may live well. But no one will be deprived of their belongings for any reason. If that happens you know what will happen?"

The smile left his face and he looked at the ground. "Yes, sir I do. We are not used to that you know. It will be hard, but if that is what you want then I want it too. Sir I will not fail you. You have given me my family back and have shown care and concern for these people and for that I will never do anything that questions your trust of me."

I knew I had won a very important contest at that time. JuJu and his men were mine in total. I gave him the order to carry on and he set to work. These are industrious beings and when they are targeted on a project, they will work their hearts out on it.

That was a good sign and one I would build on.

We worked on the city for the next week, rebuilding the wall and cleaning up the infrastructure of the place. There had been a lot of neglect over the years, but with everyone working together we had it all worked out by the end of the month.

Meanwhile I had sent a contingent back to our main base to bring the rest of our forces forward and to set the base on auto-protection while we were away.

We were well on our way to building a new world for ourselves and these beings we had liberated. I knew now the social order in this world was one of war lords and it would be by that knowledge I would set us up in our quest of conquest over the other cities across this world. The beings of this place had no idea as to what was coming at them.

Chapter Eleven

New Order Meets Old

So far, we had carried out three major offenses and had done well in them all, actually more than well. Our total losses so far have been two dead and that my friend is remarkable. We still had the giants to worry about, but right now we could hold up on that issue.

After talking to JuJu and others in the city we had learned the giants were not that many and the city we had destroyed was the only one for several hundred miles in all directions. In addition, the giants did not venture too far out from their cities. Any chance of them coming this far was nearly impossible. Our greater concern was the other nearby warlords from the other cities.

We learned there were around thirty other cities in this part of the world who were of this culture. The rest of the world was made up of several other cultures and all were separated by walls and natural barriers. The plants on the other side of the mountain range were one of the other cultures we would be dealing with. I found that to be most interesting an intelligent plant life that had some form of a relationship with biological life on this planet.

It was at this time I met her. She entered the office I had set up for myself and my staff to request a job. As she entered, I noted the way she carried herself. She was not like the other women I had seen. No, this one was confident and had purpose. She was educated and aggressive. As I watched her, I noted she was checking everything out and doing so with a great deal of detail in her actions.

I picked up the intercom phone and called the front desk. The duty officer answered and I asked him to have that young woman come back to my office for an interview. I needed to know more about her as this place was a place of never-ending intrigue and political maneuvering. She could be there for just about any reason, both good and bad.

As she entered my office, I gestured toward the chair across the desk from me. She stood there looking at me and then the chair and then back to me. She finally walked across the office and sat down facing me. She was striking with these absolutely beautiful gray eyes. You could see the intelligence behind those eyes and that told me this was no normal individual.

My mind thought back to the old base and its commander and how they had made contact with these people and had lived with them for a time. During that time, she could have well been the product of a union between the base command and the people of this planet. I was not sure, but planned on pursuing that issue as well.

I finally asked her. "What is your name?"

She sat there looking around. "Del."

I watched her as I continued. "Del, do you have people here in this city?"

Nodding her head, she turned toward me. "Yes, my mother and two brothers."

I felt myself smile and then lean forward in my chair. "Just what are you doing here today?"

She shifted her total attention to me. "I guess I'm more curious than anything else. I would like to find a job, but I don't know if I want to work here in this place among you beings."

"Is there a problem with us that you find it hard to be around?"

She was starting to become defensive at this time and even more nervous, moving around in the chair she was sitting on. "No. I didn't mean it that way. It's just that, you're strangers here and after the attack on our city and everything else, I." She stopped and sat there looking at me and then down to the desk top. "I don't know why I really came here. I shouldn't have. I'm sorry I think I should leave."

She started to get up and I waved her back down in the chair. "No. Please relax and sit down. I don't mean you any harm or unpleasantness. I just want to know how you feel about our being here, that's all.

"Look, we are trapped here after having our forces almost totally destroyed on the other side of that mountain range. By the time

219

we figured out what was happening most of our command was gone. As it turns out we come from a different dimension.

"Don't ask me how because I don't know. All I know is that we are here and this is where we will be staying. As a result, we must survive and after the experience with the plant life on the other side, we are taking no chances with any other life form on this planet.

"As I watched you come into this office, I knew that there was someone here with the ability to understand us and hopefully help us understand you and your world. So far it's been one hell of a fight just to stay alive."

She said nothing but sat there watching me and listening. I waited for several seconds and then, moving rather uncomfortably in my seat. "When I looked at you, I think I saw elements of the beings that had first occupied the mountain caves we discovered. You have their same facial features and body build. Am I right in that assumption?"

This time she started to nod her head. "You are right. Back when those being were here one had met my great grandmother and they had become one. They had several children and out of that I was eventually born. Those of us with that past heritage in us are not treated too well in this place."

Now I knew why she was so careful and distrustful of others. "Then you have been fighting to survive within this society?"

I could tell that she was starting to relax somewhat. "Yes, there are not many of us left here. It is not advisable for anyone of a pure race on this world to marry those of us who are not pure."

I needed to ask her a number of questions that could be rather difficult to deal with, but if anyone was going to be able to provide me with answers, she would be the one. Finally, I decided to go for it. "Del, I hope this question will not offend or embarrass you, but I need to ask it. We find these beings to be rather deceitful and manipulative. Is my assessment of them right in that respect?"

She sat back, looking me straight in the eyes and started to nod her head. "That is true. The ability to lie and manipulate others determines a being's place in this world. The better you are at it the higher you climb and the more power you gain. It is the normal thing in this world. Those of us who are mixed find that our ability to be deceitful is limited. However, you must know that it comes as a necessity within this world. You fail in that relationship with others and you fail in all aspects of life here. How do you know if I'm not being deceitful now?"

She was right there and at this point I had no way of knowing. However, I was not going to let her know that. I knew enough that whatever these beings said needed to be matched with their actions and their actions spoke the truth. "I don't, but in short order I will. You of this world have a hard time matching your actions to your words. Every leader I have dealt with so far has shown that trait and I doubt if you can avoid it as well."

She smiled. "And, if you find someone is being deceitful, what are your plans or what have you done in response?"

Now she was getting directly to the point and this was my opportunity to demonstrate my power and leadership. "Well, Del, to put it rather bluntly, I kill them."

That hit the target. She looked around like someone who was looking for the quickest way out of wherever they were. She then looked back at me and the story was in her eyes. She was scared, really scared. I needed to say something right then and there to ease her situation. "Del, relax. While in this office all negative actions by me or my staff is suspended. If you're being deceitful to me right now, I'll know it and will take the proper action, but I will not kill you or anyone else. What I need you to know is that I have determined that by taking these deceitful leaders head on, I can eliminate a lot of problems."

I had held my hand up to try and get her to calm down and I gave her the time she needed to relax and recognize that I was not going to take any radical action at this time. "By the way you responded I assume that you may have been a little deceitful with me at this time. Is that true?"

She was still gripping the arms of the chair and started to nod her head. She was trapped and she knew it and now she had to face the truth and be up front with me. "Sir, it is our way and even though I know it's wrong, I still tend to use it as a means of surviving. The truth is, I don't trust you or any of your beings. Yet, the same is true for my own beings here in this world. I have managed to survive by being just as deceitful as the rest of my beings are. It's not easy, believe me."

"Del, I know what you're saying. I have been learning that lesson myself and it's a hard one to learn. May I propose this to you? From this moment on you and I will be totally honest with each other, I will no longer try to trap you and I will work with you in every way keeping a trusting relationship going. Is that acceptable to you?"

She was looking down at the floor and then back up to me. I could tell she was thinking hard and trying to come up with an appropriate response. "I will try my best to keep that relationship with you. You must understand my entire life has been like this and it will not be an easy thing for me to do. That is, to be completely honest with you at all times.

"I want to, but I am not foolish enough to say that I will never do it. I know that is not the answer you want, but it's all I have right now. I would say this, if we move on in this way and you do find me becoming that way, if you tell me so I can correct myself."

She was right, how do you change something that has been your life, a permanent part of you for all your life. No, her response was right and she was trying, I had no doubt about that. I then made the proposal. "Del, how would you feel if I asked you to come to work with me, as my interpreter and liaison with your people?"

That set her back and she started looking around again. I knew I had put her in a difficult situation and would not have been surprised if she had refused. Her response somewhat surprised me anyway. "To have a close relationship with you would set me up for assassination. The beings of this city may welcome you, but they plan to eventually kill you just as they did the other many years ago." She was now looking me hard in the eyes as she spoke.

"You must remember that everything they say or do is a survival action. It is not to satisfy you or assist you, but is a means of setting things up in the future to take action against you. Time is on their side and they know it. In that time, they will kill you, each and every one of you."

Now she was being honest and to the point. I was also finding myself nodding as she spoke. When she finished, I knew it was my turn to try and convince her that I needed her and that we would protect her. "Del, I understand what you are saying and all you have said is true. I know they plan on killing us. That becomes my problem as to just how I should handle it. Right now, I have decided when I meet deceit the deceitful one will die right there and then. That has worked, but it will not solve all my problems. In the end we want to live in peace in this place. We don't want to be here, in this place, but have no way out."

Her eyes had become soft and she now understood our dilemma. She then stood up and walked over to the door, stopped and turned back to me. "I will work for you and that means I must move in here with you. I will go to my home and collect my belongings and return here this afternoon. I cannot stay at my home any longer. They will know immediately I have associated myself with you and it will be my death sentence. Is this alright with you?"

Wow, I had not thought of that, but she was right. They would kill her and now her life was in my hands. I got up from the desk and walked over to her and took her right hand with my right hand. I looked at her hand. It was small and soft and she appeared so vulnerable at that moment. "Del, I agree with what you say and I also apologize for putting you in this situation. If you want to back out then I have no problem with you pulling out. I don't want you to suffer due to our problems."

She was now watching me closely and started to nod her head. "Listen to me. My life has been one abuse after another. I have no real relationship with these beings because of my past relatives' relationship with the other beings who came here. I will never have an opportunity to have a life as a mother or a wife because of my past. I am tolerated and that is about it. If I died tomorrow, they would have forgotten all about me by the next day. No, what I do now gives me a greater chance at life than I have had in the past or will have in the future. I'll be back in about two hours."

She then smiled and left my office. As I watched her going out the front door, I found I was developing feelings toward her and I needed to guard against those feelings. She was still of this place and still had all the tendencies these beings had. It would be a hard road working with her, but I felt we could help one another adjust to each other's situation better than I could with a regular being in this place.

It then dawned on me if she was here, then there had to be others here as well. I made a mental note to talk to Del about them and get her input in how we could use them or should we. This could turn out to be an interesting situation.

I returned to my desk and started to address the actual need to build some type of a relationship with these beings whether deceitful or not. I knew muscle and power spoke louder than reason with them and I would maintain this stance for the time being. I was putting together a listing of whom and what we would be concentrating on when Brad came in. "Captain, we have a problem."

That was all I needed right now and so I set my pen down and turned to him. "All right Brad, what do you have?"

He came over to the desk and sat down across from me and leaned back. "Well, it seems that now we are in charge around here we're responsible for maintaining and running all of the cities needs and services. The citizens of this city have decided to turn everything over to us."

I sat there looking at him and thought to myself. *Here it comes, the challenge to my authority and control of these beings. I knew it was coming and I knew what I wanted to do to overcome it. Now was the time and it would be something to see.*

I then looked at Brad. "All right go out and bring all the city workers and leaders to the town square. I'll be out there in forty-five minutes on the nose."

Brad nodded his head and got up and left. He knew what was about to happen and he was not going to question it.

It wasn't more than thirty minutes later when Del came back in and knocked on my door. I waved her in and motioned toward the chair. She walked over and sat down. "They refused to come to work this morning, didn't they?"

I smiled at her and nodded my head. "Yeah, I've been expecting it and I have a solution. It may not be the right one in your eyes, but it will get the message across and will clearly lay down my expectations to each and every one of the citizens of this place."

I watched for her reaction and she showed a half smile and then sat up straighter. "I think I want to be there to see this. They don't think you'll accept their challenge and are sure they will be able to bluff you. I don't think that's going to happen."

"You sure you want to be there?"

"I wouldn't miss it for a second."

I was watching her. "It could get nasty in a rather short time. And once it starts your relationship with this city will be ended. If anything goes bad for us, it will be for you as well. Do you understand?"

She smiled. "Look, my life had little or no meaning until you and your people came along. I'm more related to your situation than to those of this city. They chose to reject me and so I have made my decision and I'm willing to die by this decision. Things could not get any worse for me than they already are."

I looked at my watch and stood up. "All right then why don't we go and see what we can do to make some people real nervous. Now listen to me, I want you to stay back and out of the way. Find a place where you can see everything, but do not get involved or question my actions, if you can, stay as plain faced as possible. It is not going to be pleasant, but it will leave a lasting impression."

We walked out the door and across to the city square. Del moved off to my right and took up a place near my command staff and against a building wall. I walked out into the square and stepped up on the landing in the middle of the square. I then turned to the crowd of beings standing to my left.

I pointed at the city mayor and asked him to step forward and when he got into position I asked. "What is this issue about running the city services? I thought that was your job."

He smiled at me like he had me in a corner. "But sir, you have taken away our authority and control and that means you accept the issue of running our city for us. It can be no other way."

I was watching him closely and noted his whole body was taught and there was a little quiver in his arms and hands. I then looked out across at the whole of the crowd standing there. I said nothing and simply pulled my .45 out and shot the mayor in the head. The place was dead silent. "Now whoever will be taking over in the mayor's place can step forward and we will discuss this issue about running the city service."

Everyone there was looking around and silently talking to one another. Finally, a man stepped forward with his hand outstretched palms up. "Sir I will take over the mayor's duties and get things back to normal operating order, if it is all right with you?"

I smiled at him. "Thank you. I'm sure these citizens of your city will be grateful for your service and interest in their welfare."

I then left the center and returned to my office and sat down to wait and see what happened next. It wasn't long before Brad and Del came in to report all the city services were being cared for and it was business as usual.

I thanked Brad and he left and Del moved over and sat down in the chair. She was a little pale and I gave her a few minutes to regain herself. "Well, what do you think?"

Her mouth dropped open and she shrugged her shoulders. "I don't know what to think. I've never seen anything like that before. That lying old trouble maker has been getting away with stuff like that for year. He sure as hell didn't this time."

I smiled. "Do you think I over reacted to his actions?"

"I think you shoved his action back down his lying throat. I don't believe anyone in the city has seen that before."

Did I make an impression?"

She nodded. "An impression, yes you did and it impressed me as well. It will be a long time before anyone even thinks about challenging you again."

"Then we can move on and start planning our next move in the coming weeks against the other cities?" I was still watching her closely. I was ready for just about anything to come from her.

She shrugged her shoulders. "I have no idea what you're planning for the other cities, but if you mean to take your presence to those other cities, I think they already know their worst nightmare is coming true. Whichever city you go after, it will be yours with little or no conflict."

"Are you sure about that?"

"Listen your action with the mayor has already reached the other cities. They know what's coming and I doubt very much they will resist you in any way.

"Second, they will also see the military from this city working with you and that will clearly give them all the reason in the world to give up. You must remember our cities are like little worlds of their own. Each one is always trying to overcome the others nearby.

"Not only that, they will be trying in every way possible to gain a position of power under you and then you can control everything they do. When these cities start to manipulate the system between one another you will see the deceit in its finest form.

"Frankly, you'll need to do nothing, just let them work it out and in time they will. The target will always be the pleasing of you."

She sat there with a smile on her face. There was an air of satisfaction about her that told me she was happy with her place in this whole mess.

"All right Del I think we're ready to take the next step."

She sat there nodding and waiting for me to continue. I started to lay out my actions and needs I wanted her to consider. "Del, starting tomorrow I need to start to find staff personnel who will be loyal to me. They must be individuals who will fall into line and carry out my orders to the letter.

"The individuals who I select must be committed to me so I can give an order to them and then leave and be sure they will in turn obey those orders. What do you think, are there any around who fit that need?"

She had been listening to me intently and when I finished, she sat there thinking over what I had just said to her. She then looked up, "Sir?"

I immediately raised my hand to stop her. "Del please listen to me I don't want this 'Sir' thing anymore, do you understand? I would prefer you call me Alexander or Alex or anything but sir, is that all right with you?"

There was a look of surprise and doubt in her face and then. "Sir, if that, I mean, Alexander, if that is what you want then I will call you by that name."

I nodded. "All right then would you please continue."

She adjusted herself in the chair and continued. "Alexander, the short answer to your question is yes there are people here with those qualities. The problem you will have is getting by the socially accepted way of doing things here.

"There is within this world an element of these beings you could call throwbacks. That is, they tend to want to be honest and straight forward in their dealing with their day to day lives. As with my kind they have developed in the norms of this society and have managed to do well over the millennia's."

That's what I needed and I had the key sitting there in front of me to finding these people and bringing them on board with me. An element within this society actually tended to be honest and straight forward in their dealing with one another which was a novel idea. "All right Del, now tell me, how do we go about finding these people and enlisting them?"

She smiled. "Alexander you already have the means of doing that. The methods you used in finding me out and addressing my needs and situation are the same methods you will used to find the others. Believe me when I tell you there are a lot of them out there just waiting for the opportunity to see changes come in this social order. No, I can assure you, you will find many of them with those qualifications and they will be honored and committed to you."

With that I picked up the phone and called Brad. In less than a minute he was in my office. "Brad, pull up a chair and join us. I think we've come up with a solution to a problem we have."

Once he was ready, I laid out the situation and what Del had just told me. "Brad, hidden within the fabric of this society was the fragments of a social order that is the opposite of what is the predominantly socially accepted acts in this current society. All we need do is identify them and bring them on board to work for and with us. Brad if we can do that then this world is ours in total and we can never be stopped or overcome, do you understand?"

He sat there a moment. "I would give my eye teeth to find a means of overcoming the system currently existing here. If there are enough of these people around then I think we have the ability to do just what we need to do. I'm ready for it. Where do we go from here?"

This confirmed what I was feeling. We were on the verge of finding the solution to a problem, if not addressed, would in time kill my entire command to the last man. It was a subculture of this current one and was in fact the opposite of this main culture. It would be a job, but if we worked it right, we could change everything and secure our future.

I had Brad and Del sitting there in front of me. One was my loyal second in command and the other an individual who had been surviving in this society for years and managing to stay alive. She lacked the deceit prevalent in this society and that made her worth her weight in gold. "All right Del I need you to start screening people for me so we can bring these people here to be interview. Can you do that for me?"

Her reply gave me just what I was looking for. "How many do you want to start out with and do you want men or women or both?"

"Del I don't care what their sex is, what I want are people who are honest and can be trusted to do their job and do it well. I want people who cannot be approached by the primary social order in this place and bought. I want people who can look these being in the face and deal with them and their methods. Know what I mean?"

She was sitting there writing down notes as I talked to her. "Alexander, I know a number of these people. We have learned to depend on one another in order to survive in this social order. They in turn know a number of people who meet the same criteria. If you wish I can contact a number of them and have them come in and speak to us or you and then see where that takes us."

That's what I needed and she had the key to my plan. I then decided I wanted to talk to a number of these people and see if I could get an idea or measure as to their value to me. "Del, would you contact six of those people and see if they can come in to see me tomorrow. If they can then I want you there with me as I interview them. You may have an insight as to whether they are what we want or not."

She agreed and made a note of the assignment. She got up and left the office to find a phone and start calling those she knew.

Brad had been sitting there watching and listening to Del and my exchange. After she left, he asked. "Can you trust her?"

I sat there looking out the window and then turned toward Brad. "I don't know Brad, but by the end of tomorrow I'll know if I made the right choice in hiring her. If not then were back to where we started. That's a bet I'm willing to take."

Brad stood up and looked at me and then nodded and turned and walked out the door. I knew what he was thinking and I agreed with his concern, this was a gamble at best or a completely stupid move at the worst. Right now, I felt Del was being honest with

me and she would in fact perform as I hoped
she would. We would know tomorrow.

Chapter Twelve

Challenging the Status Quo

I found myself up at sunup. This was going to be the test day for my new plan. If everything goes right, I will have found a new resource of people who I can trust and work with. It all depended on my reading of Del and whether she was actually different from the norm on this planet or was in fact playing the same game as everyone else, lying her teeth out about everything. If she was then she would not make it through the day alive.

I had learned with these people there was only one thing that made a mark on them and it was their personal safety. So far anyone of them would sacrifice their neighbors, friends, family and strangers in order to survive. Even Juju was still questionable.

There was no loyalty to anyone by anyone and unless I could overcome this, we were dead.

After taking my shower I walked over to my office and sat down and looked out the window. I hadn't had time over these past few weeks to actually sit down and contemplate what was going on and what had happened to us since we landed on this planet. A lot of people had died in that time and we, my unit, had been reduced to just a fraction of what we had been.

I sat there thinking about what I had been doing and whether it was the right thing to do. We had killed a lot of natives over this time frame and if things continued to go as they currently are, we will kill many more in the near future. I guess, with me I was trying to determine whether my actions were right or wrong. It's not good for one to question his motives in the middle of the game, but I found unless I did this from time to time, I tended to lose track of my goals and purpose.

In addition, I was starting to have feeling that something was wrong. I don't have any firm grasp on what that something is but it's there sitting in the back of my mind and not making any move forward for me to

242

grasp and work on. There was something about this place, something that was intangible and hiding from me. I felt it and I could almost smell it.

It crossed my mind I had been and was looking right at it but still not seeing it. The thing was really eating at me whatever this thing was it was far more dangerous than anything we had faced so far. What the hell was it anyway?

Bottom line, it was all about surviving. The next question that needed to be asked was. "Is it worth it?" That would become the premier issue as things progressed. The beings, here on this planet, were smart and cunning and they would sacrifice one another knowing in the end they would win out over those of us who were trying to overcome them.

If I was going to avoid that I had to change their entire social order. This was my target today, trying to determine if there was an element within this society that could be tapped as a means of changing the current social system.

As I sat there, I knew it was a huge gamble, one that would determine the life and death of every one of my people. They have been through hell itself and there is much more to come. The question was, were they up to it? Again, what was about to take place in this office today would determine the fate, both for my people and myself. One thing I knew, before we succumbed to this planet, I would leave a mark that would last through the ages.

I went to breakfast and found Brad sitting by himself off in a corner. As I sat down in front of him, I could see, like me, he had not slept well. His eyes were dark and there were bags under them. I sat there looking at him as he ate whatever it was, he was eating. After several seconds he stopped and looked up and me. "What?"

I raised my right hand off the table and sat back. "I don't know Brad. I think you would eat just about anything that landed in front of you. I don't know what it is your stuffing into your face right now, but I do know it's not something I want."

A smile flashed across his face and he sat up and pushed himself back from the plate. "Boss it has nothing to do with what I'm eating and everything to do with keeping my strength up and being ready to do whatever the hell you come up with next."

"OK you have me there. Has it been that bad these past few days?"

"Boss, it's not that it's been bad or anything like that. I guess the confusion that seems to radiate from everything we do lately is what is bothering me. I don't oppose what you're trying to do, I just wonder if it's the right way to go."

"You think I'm depending too much on Del in my decision making?"

He sat there looking at the plate in front of him. "To a degree I have to say yes. There are so many unknowns about her and yet you have appeared to become dependent on her and what she thinks. I still think you're on the right track, but I fear her influence on you."

That caused me to set back and start to rethink my current situation. He was right in his observation; the only question was whether that observation was as big a problem as he felt it was. "Brad I think I see what your concern is and the only way I can answer that is that I know the nature of these beings. I also know that we must overcome that nature or else we cannot survive.

"Right now, Del is the key to our success here. I know her background and I also worry about whether she is being truthful or actually playing the game that all these beings play. They are a deceitful social order and the only way to overcome that is to kill the deceit. To strike at it head on and right now my only hope of doing that is Del.

"She is a gamble and one I must play close to the chest. If my assumptions are right on, then we have beat these beings at their own game. If my assumptions are wrong, well, you and I won't have to worry much longer.

"This I can promise you, if Del proves to be just more of the same thing, she will not live through the day. I'll drag her out to the square and put a round through her head just as I would any other of these creatures. But, if my gamble turns out to be right on the money, then we will use Del and any others like her to kill this social system here and now."

He sat there looking at me. I could see his mind was running at full speed. He then picked up his fork and started running it through that stuff on his plate. "Then, you're on top of this thing and ready to deal with it?"

Nodding I placed both hands on the table top. "Yeah Brad, I am."

"OK then I'll get back to my job and wait for you to call on me for whatever it is you may need. Boss, I know you understand that we all depend on you. But from time to time, we just don't know what that mind of yours is up to." He then started eating that stuff again.

I sat back looking at this man I have found to be indispensable to my plans. If loyalty were to be measured it would be by this man's standards. I determined then and there I would not let him down. "All right Brad, as this thing develops, I'll keep you informed. Please don't plan on being out of the office today. If things go bad, I'll need to move fast and deliberately."

He raised his fork and nodded his head.

I got up and walked over to the food line and got a cup of coffee and two sticky buns and headed back to my office. As I came into the main reception area there was Del waiting for me. As I looked at her, I wondered just what this day was going to bring in relationship to her future. She had no idea as to what the stakes were at this time, but before this day was over, she would, one way or the other.

She stood up as I approached. "Alexander, I have six people coming in to see you this morning. I think they are the best of what you are looking for at this time. If you want, I'm ready to give you a briefing on each of them at this time?"

She handed me several folders and then followed me into the office. As I sat down at my desk she moved around and over to the window. I swung around in my chair and looked at her. Standing there in the window I could, for the first time, get a clear look at this person who had pushed her way into my life.

She was looking out the window with her arms folded across her chest. It struck me that she was a most beautiful creature. I could feel the desire welling up in me and knew I needed to be careful and defensive at this time. Any feelings like that would have to wait until this day was over. I could not let emotions dictate to me this day. Tomorrow she may not be here and I needed to understand that.

I reached over and picked up the first folder. As I opened it, she turned and moved back around to the chair across from me and sat down. "When will the first one be here?"

"I set a time at one o'clock for the first one. His name is Dominic. He's twenty-seven years old and fully trained in our educational system. He is not married nor is he a father.

His current work is that of a clerk and that will be the highest he will ever be able to advance in this system. Of the six he is the most committed to an ethical and moral life. Once you talk to him you will know what I mean by that." She then sat back and waited for any question I might have.

I finished reading the details on his history and then set the folder down and looked at Del. "Del is this man related to you?"

She appeared to be a little surprised by the question. "Alexander, we're all related in one way or the other. I can say by blood I don't think so, but by our social standing yes we are."

Good answer, I hadn't expected that level of skill and understanding in her. "Good, has he ever been punished under your laws?"

She nodded her head. "Yes, he has, as have most of the rest of us. I for example have been punished three times for attempting to associate with upper tier citizens. Dominic was punished for striking an upper tier citizen after being humiliated in public. He served three years of hard labor. You will see the results of that sentence when you see him. Every mark on him came during that time."

I then picked up the second folder and opened it. This person's name was Homer. He was thirty-four years old and his occupation was listed as laborer. There was no indication of his education. I looked at Del. "What about this Homer. He appears to be less educated. Is he married or what?"

She looked at me. "I can't tell you; I was not able to contact him myself. I had to go through another one of the applicants because I was not allowed in the area where he works. You need to understand many times these people are restricted in their movements and their history is restricted as well. Homer is what you would call rebellious. He hates the system and tries in every way he can to resist it.

"Frankly, I'm surprised he has not been killed by now. Normally, people of this nature are not tolerated by the powers to be, but in his case, they have not taken that route. I think they consider him insane and as a result not a danger to anyone other than himself."

I looked at her. "Does this mean he is dangerous or violent to or with others?"

"I don't think so. Everything I can find out about him is his issue is with the governing council and not everyday people.

He just does not like being walked on and driven into the ground. As a result, he is vocal about it and cares little about what they think of it. He has spent time in prison because of his rebellious attitude. Whether he will fit into your needs, I'm not sure."

I then picked up the next folder and this one addressed a woman. As I read over the information, I got the feeling this one was far more complex than either of the prior two. She was well educated and appeared to be in a rather high level of their social order. "What about this one, this Victoria?"

Del smiled. "Victoria is an old friend of mine. I'm sorry but I just could not let this opportunity pass without giving her a chance. I love her dearly and would do just about anything to help her along.

"This is probably the most patient person you will ever meet. She had made her way through this social system through pure patience and hard work. She has the ability to identify those areas where power is the key and she needed to avoid power issue. Any threat to a power base is the end of your career in this society. She knew the ins and outs of the process.

"She has built her career as a consultant. She has great common sense and it is for that which she is in demand. In this way she has had access to the highest levels of our system and has enjoyed just as high a level of respect. Yes, she is a half breed, but one who has learned to work the system and work it well. She does not possess any level of power as it is used in the upper class. But she knows how to work those who do and she's good at it."

I was reading the review on her. "Del it says here she is forty years old. That brings up a question that just popped into my mind. What is the average life expectancy here?"

"Alexander, there are two life expectancies here. One is for the half breed and the other for the rest of the social order. For the half breed the average is around fifty-seven years. The reason is that half breeds face a higher level of execution for transgressions against the social order. The average age for the normal beings is somewhere around one hundred eighty-six years. It would be higher except there is such a high level of death due to war among the men." By this time, she had stood up and walked back over to the window as she spoke.

I set Victoria's folder down and picked up number fours. I opened it and started to read. This one was named Shelah age twenty-six. The folder was the thickest of the six. As I shuffled through the papers, I noted most of what I was seeing was official forms of some kind. I looked at Del. "What do we have here Del?"

She appeared to be a little uneasy and then settled down. "Shelah, she is the most questionable one of the candidates you will be meeting. She's a hard worker, but she is there totally for herself. Whatever she does ultimately targeted is for her own benefit.

"Don't get me wrong, she is a hard worker and will do everything she can to complete a task and do it right. It's just that her ulterior motives are what are best for her first and foremost."

I looked at Del to try and determine if there was a bit of jealousy being demonstrated there but she appeared to be sincere and serious. "You think she would be a problem for us in some way?"

She looked down at the floor and then back at me and took a deep breath. "No, she would be targeting you for your favor. She would do everything in her power to push me aside and take my place even unto destroying my reputation. She has done it to others and I don't see her changing."

Her face was a little red and she was shaking some as she finished. I sat back looking at her and realized Del was scared. She had been brought in to assist me and now she was seeing the possibility she would be replaced by this Shelah.

What was even more interesting was she had included Shelah in the pile of possible employees she brought to me. I smiled and realized she had done her job and had been honest and ethical in carrying it out even if it meant she could be out of a job.

I set Shelah's file aside and looked at Del. "Del, don't worry."

She looked at me and smiled and sat back, I had a dedicated worker there and that meant everything at this time.

I picked up the fifth file and opened it. This was a twenty-nine-year-old man named Brady. He was handicapped due to a severe beating he had taken one time from a number of natives who took exception to his being at a particular location. He had lost a foot and had trouble getting around, but he was a hard worker and never gave up. "Del, why did you put this Brady in the pile?"

She looked at me. "Because he deserves something good happening to him, that's why. He has never given up and still tries his best to be the best he can be. He does not complain but instead gets back up and forges ahead.

"I don't know of anyone more deserving than Brady and that includes me. He knows he will never be permitted to advance in this society, but he still keeps working. They have never been able to slow him down and I fear one day they will kill him. He needs this opportunity and he will give you everything he has."

The sixth file was on a man age fifty-one. His name was Charles and he had a criminal record that would impress anyone. As I sat there reading over the list of crimes and punishment I was even impressed. The one thing I did notice was his crimes were always against the upper element of this social system and never included violence. He never denied any of the charges and stood in front of their court and agreed with the charges.

I looked at Del and she was looking straight at me. "He is tough as nails and will take on anything you assign him to. On top of that he knows more about the upper class in the city than anyone else anywhere. He never lies and always takes responsibilities for his actions."

I nodded my head and set the file down. "When do they start to come?"

"They will be here starting at one o'clock. I anticipated an hours' time with each one. They will come in the order you have looked at the files. Is there anything else?"

I stood up and walked around the desk and over to my office door and opened it. I then looked back at her. "Let's take a walk."

A puzzled look came to her face as she stood up and followed me out the door. I walked down the hall to the end where there was another door and opened it and walked in with Del right behind. I pointed at the chair in front of the desk and asked her to sit down. I leaned across the desk, looking Brad directly in the eyes. "Now ask her anything you want. I'm giving you sixty minutes with her and then it's done."

Brad looked a little shocked as did Del as I turned and walked back to the door and closed it behind me. I was taking one hell of a chance here, but I needed to have Brad on board all the way with these people and this was the only way I could go to achieve that end. I had fed Del to the lion and all I could do was sit there and wait.

It wasn't thirty-five minutes later when the door opened and Del came in and walked up to my desk and sat down in the chair. I sat there waiting for her to blow up but she didn't. "Why did you do that?"

She didn't appear to be mad or hurt or anything emotionally telling, but she did sound serious. "Del I have to have everyone on board with this program I am setting up. What is happening here in this city will determine yours and my survival and everyone we know and have feeling for.

"Things appear peaceful right now but I can assure you in the not-too-distant future the resistance will start. We are not in control here. We are only on top of the pile right now. We have scared them, but once that passes then the guerrilla warfare will start. The only way we can deal with it is to kill it before it gets started. I plan on doing that by getting you half breeds to join in with me to deal with the social structure of this city.

"We need to be ready so when they make their first move, we can respond and finish it then and there. This social order is based on deceit, on the big lie, and that has to change. We are about to go into a re-education of the citizens of this city, an education they will never forget."

Del was nodding her head as I laid it out for her. She was tracking with me and now understood what I was building. "Then you were satisfying concerns this Brad had concerning me, is that right?"

I turned away from her and then swung back around facing her. "That's right. Brad is my second in command and he must have a trust base in you and you in particular. Up until I took you into his office, he did not trust you and felt you were a major threat to me and our plans. I am now waiting for his response concerning you.

"Del, what he says will determine whether you remain here or not, it's that simple. If you are what you appear to be then there is nothing to worry about. However, if you are not then you're no longer here. Do you understand?"

A flash of anger charged across her face and then receded almost as fast. She sat

258

there looking at me as if I had just punched her in the face. It took her several seconds to regain her composure. "Alexander, I think I understand what you're saying. I'll be truthful with you; I was not happy when you dumped me there in Brad's office and then walked out. I felt like I had been dropped into a trap and I was about to get another lesson on deceit. I answered his questions and hopefully I did a good job, but I still felt violated.

"Alexander, my whole purpose here is to try and help you in a situation that is almost impossible to deal with. It's my chance to get out from under these beings and hopefully get to a better life than what people like me are living. I don't know if you understand that, but it's important to me and everyone like me.

"When I left Brad's office I had decided to come back here and tell you that you could take this job and stick it. I still feel that way, but right now I am beginning to understand what you're up to and I agree with it and support it. If you'll have me, I will stay and I hope Brad will approve my presence here."

I reached over and picked up the phone and dialed Brad. He answered. "Well?"

259

I sat there listening to him and after about three minutes I hung up and turned to Del. She knew the seriousness of this moment and remained quiet and attentive. What she didn't know was right then at that moment, her life had been decided. I picked up a pencil and started twisting it in my hands and then looked right at her. "He agrees with my hiring you and feels you're exactly what we need at this time and place. Now let's get ready for our interviews."

A smile shot across her face and she immediately started to pick up the file folders and moved them over to a side table. "Do you want me to stay during the interviews?"

I nodded my head. "Yes, I need you to pay close attention to their reactions as I question them. I would like you to sit in a chair over there by the window and if you have any concerns you can let me know by clearing your voice. Is that clear?"

She got up and moved a chair over by the window and then finished setting the place up as I wanted it. She then turned back to me. "Alexander, you're sure you want me in here while there here? It could cause some problems if they took my presence as a threat."

"That my dear Del is exactly what I want them to feel. I want them uncomfortable and on edge, I what their reactions to my questions to be real and raw." I had just finished clearing off my desk.

She was standing there looking at me and I assume trying to figure me out. "You really don't trust us, do you?"

I turned to her. "Del what do you expect. If you were able to put yourself into my shoes wouldn't you feel the same way? Everyone I have met in this place has been deceitful and as a result I can trust no one, not even you until I am positive you are with me and not simply trying to use me.

"My people and I did not want to be here. We were brought here and then left due to circumstances beyond our control. There is no going back for us. We either move ahead or we die. I have lost better than two thirds of my command because of this planet and I'm doing everything I can to keep the rest safe.

"Del, I'm working this thing the best way I know how. I need you and those like you, but I must also be sure you are with me and not just working me. In addition, you need me to trust you. How do you know I'm

261

not just setting you up so I can work this system for my own best results?"

She stood there listening and I could see her thinking. "Are you using us?"

"Del the answer to that is yes and no, I am using you because we need someone from this society who we can trust and right now you're our best bet. I am not using you as a means of gaining favor with those who are in control here. If this all works out then not only will my people come out on top, but we will take you and your people with us. Do you understand?"

I sat there waiting for her response. This was the one moment in our relationship when her answer would be the success or failure of our plans. I had her in a difficult position and she would have to decide right here and now as to whether she was all in or needed to drop out.

Finally, she looked up at me. "Alexander, I have worked my whole life trying to get out from under this system. My friends have paid dearly as well and some have died. We have no future here and there is no place else for us to go. No, I'm going to trust you on this and give you everything I have. If I'm wrong then I will pay with my life and frankly that would be better than continuing on like I and my friends have been.

"You're the first opportunity we've had come along to gives us any chance of getting out from under this system and we're going to work with you. I hope to hell you understand just what we are risking here?"

I had my answer and I stood up and walked around the desk to where she was sitting, reached down and took both her hands and stood her up. I then looked her in the eyes. "Del, if this thing fails it will not only be you and your friends who will die, but I and my entire command will die. This is a win or lose situation, we either come out on top or we are buried."

The connection had been made and Del was ready to really go to work. We broke for lunch and headed out of the main office building. As we walked out the front entrance, I felt it almost immediately. There was an air of quietness that literally screamed at me. There were a few people moving around on the block in front of our headquarters. I reached out and took hold of Del's arm and moved her back to the entrance and then inside. "It's starting right now."

I pulled my communicator and alerted Brad that we had an incoming attack developing and the signal went out to the rest of our forces. I had expected this and knew it would not be too long before they made their move. In short, I was ready and prepared for them.

The vehicle came around the corner to my left and started to accelerate up the street. I pressed the go button on the communicator and the suppression unit assigned to that area went into effect. The vehicle was three hundred yards from the front entry when the suppression unit struck. At first the vehicle seemed to sit there, coming to a dead stop and then it came apart at the seams. It was a perfect shot with no survivors.

Our identification units moved in and started identifying the people in the vehicle. Within fifteen minutes we had the names of the people and who they were related to or connected to in the upper level of the cities social order. I then sent out the directive to bring those people in and prepare them for interviews. Well maybe not interview, maybe just a little more aggressive than an interview. Never-the-less we would be talking to them.

I returned my attention to Del. She was a little pale, but in good shape for her first direct combat experience. As she stood there looking at the remains of the vehicle, "Del, I told you this was coming. It's as normal as breathing, they had to act and act soon. This battle is not over and until we can overcome those in the position of power and control, the problem will persist.

"That is why you and those like you are important here. We are making a change that these people will resist. What they don't understand is the change is going to take place and they either live with it or die by it."

She was nodding her head by this time and then turned back to me. "All right, now I understand and for the first time really have a grasp of just where I stand in this thing. Up until now I have been a no-body in this society and I will always be if things don't change.

"It has always been that way and always will be toward me and my kind. We have always felt that way. They could care less about me or my kind and that makes everything different now. I don't think you'll have a problem with any of my kind from here on out."

265

Chapter Thirteen

The Beginning of the Rebellion

"Have they started planting yet?" He was looking right at his second in command expecting an answer.

"Yes, we started two days ago. At the present pace the planting will be done in about two weeks' time. If all goes well the harvest will take place in three months. It will then take two months to outfit and educate them." He hoped his answer would be what his Lordship wanted to hear.

The room fell quiet as the Lordship sat there thinking over what he had been informed of. He looked across the room at the people who were his loyal followers and then sat back and started to smile. "Good, then we should be ready to strike in about six months from now, is that right?"

His second in command nodded. "In that time, we will be ready to take on these animals who have invaded our land and we will kill them to the last being."

There was an air of confidence in the room and everyone present was feeling the surge of success and triumph in their plans as they developed. His Lordship was more than a little pleased. For once he would be able to take an action that would make his position in the city solid for the rest of his life. He would be the prime ruler of the city and all others would have to submit to his will and desires. For the first time he was on the verge of achieving his goal, a goal he had been striving for over thirty years.

"All right then we are now ready to start the harassment tactics we have set up. Did the first car go out this morning?"

"Yes, your Lordship it went out right on schedule. But there is a problem. It never made it to its target. They intercepted it and destroyed it before it could reach the building. All hands were lost Lordship." He was half expecting the see his life's blood spilling onto the floor in front of him.

The Lordship sat there thinking about what had just been said and a smile came across his face. "Good, that tells me a lot about their leader. He anticipated our move and that will be important for us in the future. The game is called chess and this one knows how to play it.

"You know what chess is, don't you? It's one of the games the others brought with them when they came to live with us. It's a game of strategy and subterfuge, a game of the minds and a contest of the wills.

"I find myself matching my skills against this being and his command. Unfortunately, he will never be able to outsmart me. Every move he makes will bring him closer to the end, the end I have planned for him. I think I want him alive when it all comes to an end. I saw how he handled Denmen at the city gate that day and I plan on doing the same with him.

"By the way, when will the other Lordships be here?"

"My Lordship they plan on being here at one o'clock. The dining hall has been set up and all is ready for your conference. We have learned their leader will be conducting a number of interviews of half breeds starting at one and he will be tied up for six hours. You may be interested in this, Shelah has been invited to be interviewed and we directed her to go."

His Lordship seemed a little surprised at the notion someone had taken the initiative to have Shelah go for the interview. That person is getting a little to power happy and he did not like it. "Who made that decision to send her to the interview?"

People started looking around at each other. They knew with that question; his Lordship was not happy with what had taken place. He sat there patiently waiting for the decision maker to step forward. No one moved no one even looked at his Lordship.

He remained silent and sat there waiting and finally his second in command stepped forward. "My Lordship I made that decision. I didn't think it was something important to garner your attention. I was trying to expedite this situation because I thought having one of ours involved could bring us considerable intelligence."

The room was heavy with silence as his Lordship sat there looking at his second in command. Something like this had not been done in years and now Mark had crossed the line. His second in command had been a loyal worker for him and had never in the past shown even the slightest indication he would step out on his own and make a decision of that magnitude without first clearing it with the Lordship. "Mark you surprise me with that action. I never thought you would do anything behind my back. It raises serious concerns about your loyalty to me. Do you understand?"

"My Lordship in no way was I trying to be disloyal to you. I have dedicated my entire adult life to you and I would never do anything that would jeopardize your position or authority."

The sweat was pouring off him by this time. He had suddenly realized he had made a grave error and his very life was on the line. "Sir, there was no attempt on my part to do anything that would harm or weaken your position. I ask my Lordship what I can do to make that clear to you and to correct the error I have made."

His Lordship sat there watching his number two go through the agony of the error he had made. Yes, it had been the right thing to do, but he should have cleared it with His Lordship first. He then continued. "Mark you have been a loyal and hardworking subject and I recognize that, but what you have done is something I cannot let pass. I value your dedication to me and for that I will not take your life, but you must pay for your error.

"I have decided you will return to the line as a soldier for the next two weeks. During this assignment I want you to learn to take orders and to bring issues beyond your position to those over you. If you are successful in doing that then I will return you to the position you now hold. Is that understood?"

Mark was standing there knowing he was being humiliated and he had a choice. He had a choice either accept the punishment and live or he rejected it and died. Not much of a choice but at least he had a choice. He nodded his head. "Yes, my Lordship I accept your kindness."

His Lordship gave a small gesture with his right hand and Mark bowed and backed away from the desk and then turned and walked out the door. After he had left His Lordship waved the next in command to his desk with his left hand and leaned forward. "See that he is assigned to the most hazardous details that are to come. I don't want him to survive the next two weeks. Do you understand?"

His new second in command smiled and nodded his head and then turned and walked out of the office to see that Mark was assigned to the right team for the coming two weeks. He walked up to Mark and put his hand on Mark's left shoulder. "Damn that was spooky as hell. How do you feel?"

Mark looked at the new second and nodded his head. "I was lucky. He could have had me killed on the spot. At least this way I have a chance of surviving."

Mark then stopped and turned and looked the new second in the eyes. "Where did he send me?"

The new second looked at him. "You'll be assigned the front line in all actions against the aliens. That includes suicide bombs and everything."

Mark bowed his head and nodded. "Yeah, I knew he would be doing that. I really blew it. Let it be a lesson to you while you try to please him. Which team am I assigned to?"

"You'll go to team five. You're the bottom man and will receive all the bad news jobs first."

Mark nodded again and turned and walked off. Just that fast he had lost favor with His Lordship and now he would pay the price. He determined he would go out with courage and determination.

The planning had been completed and the different teams set about getting ready for their assault on the aliens. They were looking back those many years to the last aliens who had come to their city and what they had done to them. It would be a major fight, but in the end, they would kill each and every one of them.

Over at the garden, the planters were finishing up the final row of planting. The new crop would be up and ready in short order and they needed to get everything put together in order to meet the time limit that had been placed on them. All they hoped was the attack teams could keep the aliens busy while they finished the task at hand.

It takes a lot of work to grow an army, one that is able to drive the aliens back to their caves and then to their deaths. His Lordship wanted a million and that was what he was going to get. The factories were working overtime to produce the uniforms and weapons as the harvest progressed. Each

273

weapon and each uniform would be placed with each new fighter. Just a few months and it would be all over.

Back at His Lordships headquarter the other gang leaders had assembled in the dining hall. They were enjoying a good meal and conversation when His Lordship stood and got everyone's attention. "Friends I am most appreciative of your taking time to join me for this meal. But there is something more pressing I need to address with you and so, if it is permitted, I would like to venture directly into the issue."

All heads were nodding. Each of them knew what they were there for and they wanted to get this thing going. With that His Lordship started. "As you know we have visitors here in our city. They are the same visitors we had those many years ago except they are more violent and destructive than those of the past. We have been able to move them into a feeling that they have control of us and that is good. Now we must prove to them they do not have control; they have what we have given them.

"A short time ago I gave the order to plant a new army. That activity is currently in the process. In a few short months we will have a new million fighter army ready to take these aliens down.

"In the mean time we must keep them busy so they do not discover what we are up to. That means we must engage them in a guerrilla style war for the time being. It will mean the loss of a number of our fighters, but that sacrifice will give us the time we need to outfit the new army.

"Right now, we have a shill sitting in on an interview with the leader of the aliens. When she is finished, she will report back to me and provide everything she could gather from her meeting with this alien leader. Our target is to get to understand his personality better. Right now, we know he is a beast and will kill at a second's notice. A lot of our citizens have fallen at his hands and that is going to come to an end.

"With that I request you provide me with attack teams so we may start a continuous guerrilla war with them in order to keep them busy. I know we will be sacrificing these fighters, but the aliens must be preoccupied for the period of time we will need to produce the army.

"Right now, we feel we will need fifteen teams. I have already assigned the first

275

two teams to attack the headquarters building. The first team failed to get to the building but the second team is moving in right as I talk. If their leader is any kind of a leader he has and will expect these actions and we must not let him down.

My second here will record any teams you assign to us and you will be kept in the chain of communications as to their use and disposition. Do I have your assistance?"

He stood there waiting for the gang leaders to make up their minds. Normally this was not a topic any of them would be involved in. They were usually at each other's throats vying for a stronger position within the city. Gang warfare was their normal mode of operation and now this leader was asking them to set all that aside in order to deal with a mutual problem.

Finally, the first of his guests stood and looked at the rest of the gang leaders. "I find it difficult to be here and find I am to be working with the rest of you, but I recognize the problem we are faced with and understand for once in our lives we must stand together to deal with a mutual problem."

He then turned to the Lordship. "I will dedicate five teams to your needs and as need be, I will assign additional teams as the situation calls for it."

His Lordship nodded his head. "That my friend is most generous. I thank you and stand beside you against this threat we all face."

In short order every other gang leader stood and pledged a number of teams to the Lordship for the fight that was being initiated against the aliens. They all knew if and when they were successful, they would be faced with dealing with the Lordship as he makes his move to take over the whole of the city. That would mean a second battle would follow the first the moment the aliens were destroyed. They all stood there looking around the table knowing the coming battle was just the beginning.

The word went out to the respective gangs and the gathering started. It was during this time when Shelah returned to His Lordship to report about her meeting with the alien leader. She walked into his office and stood there before him. Though she was a half breed His Lordship had shown favor to her and he had come to depend on her for the information she was so good at gathering. "What have you child?"

277

She smiled. "I have this leader dead cold in my hands. He thinks he knows us and he can control us, but he is so wrong. I made sure he did not hire me at this time. It was too dangerous for our current plans to have me under his control. I would have found it hard to communicate with you and besides the other half breeds know who I am and they would have informed on me."

He sat there looking at her. She had been the best weapon he had ever come across. She could go anywhere and carry out his wishes without hesitation and it was accurate and detailed. "All right let's get together with my top commanders and lay this situation out. Are you ready?"

She smiled. "Yes, I am but first I need to get the film developed so you can see what their headquarters looks like. I should have that done in the next hour, is that all right?"

His Lordship smiled at her. "Yes child, you prepare the pictures and when you're done return here and I'll have my staff here and ready."

She turned and left and as she walked out the door, he thought to himself. There is value in some of these half breed after all. Too bad she'll never survive this battle.

Chapter Fourteen

The Interviews

We had the first attempt at a terrorist attack on our headquarters and I still had the interviews coming up at thirteen hundred hours. But, between that time and now I needed to talk to Brad and see how things had worked out. I found Brad in the back courtyard giving directives to the team leaders as they headed out to find the people, we had developed the list on.

As I walked up behind him, he was turning around and saw me. "Boss you had this nailed almost to the day. The rig was full of explosive and could have leveled the building if they had gotten into position. We caught them flat footed. The teams are just now heading out to make the pickups you felt would be needed. We should have everyone rounded up by this evening. When do you want to start to talk to them?"

I was more than happy with the way my people had responded. I walked up to Brad and put my right hand on his shoulder. "Damn good work here. I'm proud of the whole outfit. As far as the people we're after, lock them up for the night and we'll start talking to them in the morning. Right now, I have a number of people to interview. This couldn't have happened at a better time. I think it told the half breeds that their lot was with us if they ever wanted to be free of this social hell hole."

Brad laughed and started to turn. "We'll have every one of these people in custody and ready for you in the morning. I think this will be most interesting. One thing for sure, we're learning a hell of a lot from this bunch and the next city will be that much easier."

Brad headed off to follow up on his people's assignments. I turned to Del and then checked my watch. "Those friends of yours should be here any time now, so let's go meet them and see what happens."

With that we returned to my office and prepared for the interviews.

Dominic arrived at exactly thirteen hundred hours. He was a calm appearing person and failed to offer me his hand as he approached the desk. He moved in front of the chair and sat down all the time keeping his eyes on my eyes. There was a look of distrust and an element of fear in his eyes. He sat back and waited for me to address my needs.

I set his folder down on the desk top and started to walk around from behind my desk. As I moved around the desk, he never took his eyes off me. This was a man who trusted no one, at least until he had determined their threat level to him.

As I walked around the desk, he turned in the chair keeping an eye on me until I moved behind him and then he had to shift a hundred eighty degrees in order to maintain eye contact with me. I kept walking until I got around to the front of the desk and then I turned and sat down on the corner of the desk still watching him.

By this time, he had leaned forward in the chair and had reached out and was gripping the edge of the desk in anticipation of having to move or react in some manner.

I looked over at Del and she shrugged her shoulders and sat still.

I then leaned toward this young man. "Your name is Dominic?"

He didn't say a word but nodded his head yes in response to my question.

"You're associated with or familiar with Del?"

Again, he nodded his head and then took a quick look back at Del.

"Do you trust Del?"

Again, he nodded.

"Why did you come here?"

Finally, a question he had to answer verbally. "I came because Del asked me to."

"Do you know what this interview is all about?"

"I understand it's for a job?" He replied

"Do you know who I am?"

"Yes."

"Dominic, are you afraid of me?"

He looked back at Del and then started to nod his head. "I don't know who you are and everything I have seen or heard about you and your people has been violent and deadly. I fear I may have done something that will warrant me being killed."

This kid was scared half to death and so I needed to relieve some of that fear. "Dominic, didn't Del inform you as to what the job was and who you would be working for?"

He again nodded. "Yes, sir she did, but I can't take any one's word. We live in a dangerous place and one's word is something no one risks their life on."

Good point, at least he was thinking in the survival mode. Still, I needed to get him to relax. "Dominic, are you telling me you can't trust what I'm saying to you?"

He was clearly not gaining on his fear levels and I knew I needed to do something to give him some relief before he passed out on me. I was still waiting for his response and finally. "Sir, I have no idea what you're doing here.

"We were living the life we are used to and then the next thing we know you have invaded our city and started to kill our leaders. Because of my position here in the city I felt I was of no use to you in any way and you would, in time, come and kill me too."

I reached over and put my left hand on top of his left hand. At the same time his eyes shifted to what I was doing with my left hand and then returned to my eyes. "Dominic, I need you to listen to me. You are here to be interviewed for a job and nothing else. You will leave here alive and well. No one here is going to either harm you or take anything from you. Do you understand?"

He seemed to relax a little at that point and then sat back in the chair. "Yes, sir I understand. It's just that in my world my life depends on everything I do every day and if I cross anyone it could end at that moment without warning. It's been this way all my life and I can't help myself."

I smiled at him and patted his hand and then got up and moved back around to my chair. As I sat down, "Dominic I understand what your life has been like. Del has filled me in on your situation and how you have managed to survive. What I have you here for is to offer you the opportunity to help me build a new life here in this place. A life that gives you the chance to reach for and achieve your dreams whatever they may be. Do you understand that?"

Again, he was nodding his head.

I continued. "Now, if I offered you a job could I trust you to do your best and to be faithful and above all else be honest with me and those of my command including Del and any others of your world who may come to work for us, do you understand that?"

He took a quick look at Del and then back to me. "You're saying you may be offering me a job working for you here in the city?"

I nodded my head. "Yes, that is exactly what I am saying."

He was thinking now. "What would I say to the leaders of the city when they demanded I do something for them?"

I smiled and sat back. "You would tell them to go to hell and if they didn't like it, they could come and see me."

His eyes brightened up. "Really, they would have to see you and could not tell me what to do or where to go?"

"Dominic if you come to work for me, you will be working for me and not the city leaders. If they have any problems with that or questions then they would see me. I can assure you if you're doing the job, I have directed you to do, I will deal with them directly and if need be harshly. Do you understand me?"

He was now on the edge of the chair and gripping the front of the desk again. It was clear he could see what this all meant. He would no longer be under the thumb of those in power and would have a power base standing behind him as well. "I don't know what to say. Are you actually going to hire me or are you just kidding me?"

I leaned forward toward him. "Dominic can you be faithful and committed to me? Can you do as I instruct you to do and work hard to carry out every job, I give you?"

He was nodding his head again. "Yes, I can do that, but I have a problem." He stopped and looked at Del and then back to me. "I don't know if I can kill anyone."

I raised both my hands. "No Dominic that would not be one of your jobs. We are looking for those who can help guide us in the dealings with the powers who control this society. We are looking for policy makers and program developers who will face down these current cultural issues and help us reinstitute and move back to a moral and ethical standard within this society."

He calmed down and settled back in the seat and waited, after several seconds. "All right, I understand what you're telling me.

I'm sorry for misunderstanding you, but I have real feelings about the taking of life and that has made my life most difficult. I find it hard to trust anyone who is of the military mentality. It has nothing to do with you not being a native, it has everything to do with what you do and what you are planning on doing.

"I cannot be a part of the taking of anyone's life whether it is any of your people or my people. However, if I can help in bringing about better relationships and understandings between my people and you then I wish to be a part of this."

That was the answer I was looking for. This was a mild-mannered man and he lived the life he preached. There was a noble demeanor to him and he had a highly developed ethics. In short, he would do just fine. "All right Dominic I think we can use you. If you are in agreement then I would like to have you come to work here in this building starting tomorrow. Do you understand?"

He nodded his head.

"You will talk to Del here and she will tell you the time and location where you are to report. If you have no other questions then I

287

thank you and welcome you to our organization."

I stood up and he did the same. I offered my hand a second time and this time he took it. It was a firm and committed hand shake and I knew this man would work out well.

The next one up was Homer. As he entered my office, I could see this man too had that appearance that all half breeds seemed to have. I don't know, I guess I would call it a survival look. You know someone who has been through the most difficult of times and has come out still intact.

I directed him toward the chair and as he approached, I offered my hand which he took immediately. Again, a firm grip and I had the sense he was well experienced in dealing with all types of people or situations.

As he sat down, "Homer, do you know why you're here?"

He looked at me. "Captain Alexander, I believe I am here for an interview for a job. The nature of that job I do not know, but I am interested in it and willing to hear you out and to answer any of your questions."

Well now, we have one who is direct and exceptionally confident in his position or situation. He knew my rank and used it appropriately. That meant he either had military experience or has done his homework.

"Homer, what do you think I am going to offer you as far as the kind of job I'll be offering?"

He looked down at the floor and I could see a slight smile flash across his face. He then looked up at me and with a smile. "Captain Alexander, I know that you are trying to develop some means of dealing with the social order of our society here in this city. I believe you are trying to come up with ways and means of dealing with the deceit that is a part of this society."

Yes, this was a man who knew what was going on and had every one of the players pegged as to who was who. He was without a doubt the most confident being I have met on the planet except maybe for Del. No, he was beyond Del.

This one I would meet head on. "Homer, you know full well what is going on here and what is at stake. So, I'm going to cut right to the subject. I need natives who are willing to work for me in dealing with the social foundation of this city. My goal is to reinstate moral and ethical practices back into this society.

"That, as you know full well, is going to be one hell of a job. But if we are going to make any headway in our chances of surviving this world, we will need to change the structure of this society. That sir is what you are here for.

"Now if you are willing to work for me in this venture then we can clearly stop this chess game and get right to the bottom line. The best way to do that is to ask you straight out. Are you willing to work for me in whatever capacity I assign you to, that being the task of assisting us in the social rebuilding of this society?"

He was now sizing me up and trying to measure my level of commitment to this issue. There was a lot on the line for him, but I also could see he was measuring the advantages to him and what he had lived through all his life. He then looked right at me. "It is clear, Captain, that you need me and others like me to give you an inside understanding of these people and the system they have developed. I don't mind the idea of assisting you and working for you, but I am concerned about my welfare and those of the others you are considering once our usefulness to you has ended. That may mean little to you, but for us it will mean our lives. I guess what I am concerned about is just how far your loyalty to us, me, go in this relationship?"

That set me back and I had frankly not thought about it. He was right about his concern and he had put me right in the middle of the frying pan. My next comment would make or break this project and I needed to be right about my feelings and attitude toward these people.

Was I just wanting them as a means of fulfilling my plan and then just dumping them or was I honestly concerned for their welfare? My entire command and power base were on the line and I had better be up front and direct with this man.

I sat there looking at him and then leaned toward him. "Homer you have just addressed the primary issue of this whole mess I find me and my command sitting in the middle of. That is the question of trust and loyalty. I have always demanded loyalty of my command personnel and I punish fast and hard when there is a breach in my trust of anyone working under me.

291

"My problem now is to give you an answer you can accept and recognize as the truth and a commitment by me to you and those I hire today. It's easy to say yes, but that does not communicate the commitment from me to you and in this case, from you to me. That has to come in the acts of carrying out our duties and assignments.

"The only thing I can tell you is my loyalty to you and the others is measured by your loyalty to me. Homer, it's a reciprocating process. You show and demonstrate your loyalty to me and in turn I show and demonstrate my loyalty to you.

"So, with that I can tell you this. No one, not a single individual, not one-half breed, will be abandoned by this command ever. If you come along side of me then we both stand firm together. That does not mean we will not have disagreements, we will, but we will also work our ways through those disagreements to a just and mutually beneficial determination. Do I have your commitment?"

He sat there looking at me and then stood up and walked over to the door and stopped and then turned back toward me. He stood there looking at me and then looked over at Del and then back to me. He then walked back to my desk and reached out with his hand to shake mine. I took his hand. "If you want me, I'm yours. I can only give you my word I will honor our relationship and will give you the best counseling I am capable of. If you are hiring, I accept."

I took his hand. "Sir, I am hiring and you are hired here and now. Please see Del about time and place to start."

He nodded his head and turned and walked to the door as Del opened and followed him out.

I had just seen one of the most self-assured individuals of any in this whole damn world of theirs. Homer would be most valuable in dealing with this social structure. One thing I was sure of, I was going to have my hands full with the three I had already hired. I didn't know if I could handle all of them. What was to come would change my mind.

Chapter Fifteen

Victoria's Revelation

So far, my interviews and hiring had gone well. Dell had been right about these people they were clearly wanting a better life for themselves and were willing to work for it. My next interview was due shortly so I had to get my head back on straight. This one was a woman and apparently a favorite of Del's.

Victoria was a stately person. When she came through the door, she stood up straight. There was this calmness about her that told me this woman knew herself well and she could deal with whatever came at her.

I got up and walked around the desk to her and offered my hand. She took it in a manner that told me this was a lady, but she was a tough lady as well. I gestured toward the chair and she walked by me and moved in front of the chair and sat down.

As I walked back around the desk, she turned her head and watched me as I resumed my seat and picked up the folder on her. There was not the slightest hint of concern or worry about her face or demeanor. She was calm and in full control. I looked up at her and she smiled at me as if she was saying, 'All right, let's get this show on the road.'

I found myself clearing my throat before I started to talk. "Victoria, do you understand your reason for being here in this office?"

She slowly nodded, "Fully sir."

Short and to the point, that's interesting. "Do you have any questions before I start the interview?"

She smiled. "No, but I'm sure there will be plenty as we progress, don't you think?"

I nodded. "Yes, I'm sure there will be."

I sat there watching her and then tossed the folder onto the desk top and leaned toward her. "Enough of this game playing, Victoria, Del has filled you in on the nature of the job and work we are planning. What I need to know is what you think you could give to this program as a means of ensuring our success?"

Evidently this was what she was looking for because she sat up and then opened up on me. "Sir I'm a forty-year-old woman with no family and no prospects of having a family. I have never had the opportunity to have a family because of my half breed status in the community. If half breeds try to pair up it usually means a life of poverty and discrimination from the rest of society and sir it is legal here.

"This is a society that has grown over the last seven hundred years from a hard-working value based social structure to a degenerate self-serving social structure. There are no rules of conduct, what rules do exist are set up by those in power as a means of keeping them in power.

"It means whatever level you are born in, is the level you will die in. It makes little or no difference what you do to improve your knowledge and skills. You will remain as you were born.

"Now I do not blame those who are in the positions above me, but I do blame the process in which this social structure got here.

Would you like to hear and learn about the process that brought us to this point?"

That set me back but it was something I felt was vital at this time. I had sitting there before me an individual who was well educated and had an in-depth knowledge of this world and how it became this way. Yes, I needed to hear her out. "Please Victoria, tell me about it."

She then looked over at Del and sat up in her chair, I saw her grip the arms of the chair. "Let me start about eight hundred years ago. The world had entered into an industrialization phase and the growth in technology was moving at a fantastic rate. Almost daily people were coming up with new ideas and machines and products and the social structure of the world changed along with it.

"For the next hundred years this growth continued and eventually moved on into the electronics age. It was during this time that computers, telecommunications, weapons of war, medical and health improvements started to be developed. People had more time to themselves and their families. There were rules of conduct both from a legal perspective and from a moral and ethical perspective. It was a time when every human being was able to strive for and reach their dreams.

"This time frame also brought about changes which started to take place in the social order of the time. Schools of higher education started to teach and encourage students that there were no rules. They were taught they could and should do as they felt and desired and not what was expected of them.

"There were no limits on what you could or wanted to do. This brought society into a time of social revolt where the moral and ethical standards of the time were directly challenged by the new social order coming out of our schools.

"We were facing huge changes in our climate and there were wars being fought all across the face of the world. It was not just political issues these wars were being fought over it included religious and philosophical issues as well. The face of the world was changing both physically and socially and a lot of people were dying.

"Human activity that had been barred as morally bad was now being presented as normal human activity. It started with chemical uses then referred to as drug abuse.

In short order most drugs were made legal and the population went on a drug use binge, again with millions dying. Along with that came the sexual revolution where the acts and sexual orientation that had been deemed immoral was being declared normal acts of nature.

"Once the sexual orientation of the social structure of society had been changed, it spread across the face of the world and with that change in the sexual orientation the destruction of the family unit was not far behind. That was the bases of our social foundation. Not far behind came the legalization of prostitution. It was deemed a proper form of occupation and that those who entered that occupation would be well paid and cared for.

"As the social system degenerated and the individual became central to the purpose for living other sexual orientations had once been seen as unhealthy and morally damaging started to demand their recognition. Polygamy soon became an accepted norm and that was followed by other beliefs all related to sexual desires.

It was a hundred years after this overall change started the final step and death of moral and ethical standards came. This brought about the recognition and legitimization of the Pedophile. At that point the children of the world became a target for total sexual exploitation.

"Finally, a great war broke out and billions died as a result of the nuclear holocaust that followed. It not only decimated the world's population it changed the climate as well.

"Areas that had been lush were now desert and the reverse. Where governments had once been there was now anarchy, a governmental system that many schools of higher education had supported and indoctrinated their students in.

"The resulting world is what you have found here. Across the face of the world there were small social orders controlled by people of power and the means of using it. In addition, due to the nuclear weapons used, there were areas where living beings and creatures were affected by the radiation and have gone through significant physical changes. You have met some of them in the giants and the intelligent plant life on the other side of the mountain range.

"In the end you have what you found here, a world out of control and in the process of dying. It's a place where care and concern for others has been replaced with a predatory environment. Where one social order fights to maintain control and dominance of all others within its area of control, a social order based on the lie and hate. It's a social order that will kill you just because of your physical history and nothing else. It's a system of slavery and deceit where the human life is of little or no value.

"This is a world that understands only one thing and that is power, power that is used with an air of ruthlessness and commitment and is so overwhelming and destructive it numbs the mind. If that level of power were to confront this world then those using it could carry out any social, moral or ethical change they desired.

"Sir, there is nothing in this world that is worth saving as far as social norms go. There needs to be an overhaul of the social orientation of this world and it needs to be done with ruthlessness beyond anything they, those in power now, have ever seen. The alien beings who came before you and were our parents failed to see that and they died for it.

No sir, if you desire change it must be total and it must be complete, it must be ruthless."

I was stunned by what she had just said. The fact was I could hardly think of anything else to ask her. Finally, it came to me. "Victoria can you tell me this? You have referred to this place as 'The World' but that does not seem right to me. Is there another name for this planet?"

She again looked over at Del and then back to me. "Yes, there is. It is a name that has not been used for many hundreds of years, but it was once the universally recognized name of this planet. That name is 'Earth' the third planet from our Sun and one of eight planets in this solar system."

Shock is not the right word for what I was feeling at this moment. That name burned its way through my mind causing me to start to shake all over, Earth? That is where I was from only it was in a different dimension than this one. Our task force had ventured out from Earth to challenge an alien force and somehow, we crossed over into another dimension and found Earth. This place was Earth after having gone through an apocalypse like none other I could ever dream of.

Del could see my reaction and she stepped forward and leaned over in front of me. "Alexander, what is it? What has Victoria said that is bothering you?"

I looked at Del and then reached over and picked the phone up and called Brad. When he came on line I said. "Brad my office, now."

I hung up the phone and then looked at Del and then back to Victoria. I waved Del back and away from me and then looking at Victoria. "Victoria you're telling me this planet of yours is named Earth, is that right?"

By now Victoria was confused and not sure as to what she had done and whether she should say anything else. I saw that in her and raised my hand. "Victoria, you're not in trouble. You have said something that will change everything for us, but I need to be sure of that. Now, did you say the name of this planet is Earth?"

She started to nod her head. "Yes sir, I did."

I then slowed down and continued. "All right now, can you tell me what continent or nation we are on right now?"

She looked at me and then seemed to understand what I was asking. "This land was known, before the great war, as the North American Continent and the country was the United States of America."

Just then Brad entered the office and stood there in the door way, gun in hand, looking straight at me, "You all right?"

I waved my hand and nodded my head and told him to put the gun away. I then motioned him over to the chair next to Victoria. "Brad, sit down. Something has happened here that you need to hear. Please let Victoria finish what she is going to tell us."

I then turned to Victoria. "Please tell Brad what you just told me about this planet and continent."

She turned to Brad and repeated what she had said to me. When she finished, she looked back at me again with a bewildered look on her face. I nodded my approval of what she had said and then turned my attention to Brad.

He was clearly trying to deal with what she had said to him. His eyes were fixed on the top of my desk and his hands were gripping the arms of the chair. He then looked up at me. "Bullshit, that's all a bunch of crap."

I sat there watching him trying to deal with the truth of what she had said. I felt sorry for the guy because this was hitting him cold and he was having one hell of a time dealing with it. I then nodded my head. "Brad it's the truth. Everything falls into place now. This is planet Earth but it's in a different dimension than the one we came from. I can't explain it to you, I'm still trying to deal with it on my own, but I believe her."

The room fell quiet as we looked at one another and then looked over at Victoria who was clearly in a state of confusion. All she could do was look back and forth between the two of us. "I don't know just what it is I have done, but it appears I have done something serious and I apologize for that. I hope this does not damage my being hired."

Finally, I got my senses back and realized what she was saying. I raised my right hand to stop her from talking. I then shifted my position and looked right at her. "Victoria you are not in trouble. What has happened here is not of your making and I can assure you I appreciate everything you have said. I can tell you right now you are hired and that I will need your knowledge and experience in the coming days as we deal with the information that you have given us."

She visibly relaxed and sat back in her seat. I then looked over at Del and waved her over to the desk. "Del would you please take Victoria out and set up the hiring paperwork and schedule her back here tomorrow or the first day she is available?"

Del nodded and reached over and put her hand on Victoria's shoulder. Victoria got up and looked at me and smiled and then bowed her head and turned and walked out with Del.

I looked over at Brad. He was still trying to deal with what had been said. "Brad you, all right?"

He shifted his eyes toward me and sat there looking at me and then started to nod his head. "Yeah, I'm OK, it was a little more than I had expected. You sure she's telling the truth?"

"I'm positive she is Brad."

We sat there maybe another forty-five seconds before he finally stood up and started to pace back and forth. "Then we are home, on planet Earth, accept we're in another dimension." He said as he shook his head.

"That my friend about describes it to the letter. This place is somewhere around five hundred years ahead of us in time. Enough time so the social changes Victoria was talking about could take place. We are in a world whose primary form of government is anarchy.

"Not only that, but it has advanced into city states much like the early Greeks back on our Earth. They have probably separated themselves out from one another based on physical mutations that were the result of the big war she was talking about. God only knows what kinds of mutations are out there. We've seen intelligent plant life and giants, so what else is there?

"This city does not appear to have any mutations but when I stop and think about it there clearly is a mutation and it's the social make up. The human traits of honesty, truthfulness, and morality are missing and what are left are animal traits and they are well developed.

"That explains the issue with the half breeds. Their parents were made up of females from this planet and males from the alien contingent who landed here. The moral and ethical traits of the aliens became dominant in the half breeds, making them an altered being compared to the people of this city. That in turn made them a minority as well as being fathered by the alien invaders.

"In time the hate and corrupt normalcy of the city dwellers overcame the aliens and they were killed off. Why they didn't kill the half breeds I don't know yet, but I will in time."

Just then Del opened the door and leaned in. "Your fourth interview is here. Should I have her wait or do you want her now?"

I looked over at Brad. "You want to sit in on this one?"

He was already nodding his head. "Yeah, I think I want to hear what is going on. Things are going to get nuts around here in the not-too-distant future and I think I better be up on things."

I nodded my head at Del and she closed the door. About twenty seconds later she opened the door and a young woman stepped in. As she came through the door, she looked at Del almost with a smirk on her face. Del was remaining neutral as best as she could but I could see the animosity between the two of them. "Alexander this is Shelah." As she said that she pointed Shelah toward the chair across from me.

As she moved across the office, she looked over a Brad and smiled at him and then turned and walked over to him and shook his hand and then turned back to me and sat down in the chair. I leaned over and offered my hand and she took it but said nothing. I glanced at Brad and he raised his eye brows and I then turned back to Shelah.

I sat back down and picked up her file and opened it. She was twenty-six years old about five feet seven and had blue eyes and brown hair. She had a hard face, but a face she could soften if and when it suited her best interest. Of the three prior interviews I felt this person was more like the city dweller than any of the others. I would need to test her honesty and moral make up before I was through with her interview.

I decided to go straight at her. "Shelah why are you here?"

She looked at me and then over to Brad and then back to me and shrugged her shoulders. "I thought you were going to tell me what I'm here for."

I was taking a dislike of this person real fast, but needed to pursue the interview if for no other reason than to get a measure on a half breed that appeared to be more on the city dweller side of the spectrum. "Didn't Del advice you as to what this interview was all about?" I looked over at Del and she nodded her head.

Shelah spread her hands with the palms up. "Yes, she did but sometimes you can't really believe or understand what Del is saying. She has a hard time making herself clear and understandable."

I looked over the top of her file and then asked. "You're here so you must have formed some idea as to what this was all about?"

She was starting to shift in her seat. "Well yes but sometime people don't tell you the truth or they leave part of the message out. You can't trust anyone around here."

"Then from what you have said so far I can't trust you or what you're saying to me now?"

She didn't like that and shot back. "I don't lie. I have a reputation of being above board on anything and everything I have worked on or dealt with. Go ahead, check my records and you will find I'm far and away ahead of anyone you have interviewed so far or have working for you." She shot a look at Del and then turned back to me.

"What do you have against Del. Besides that, what do you have against me and this command?"

She was really nervous by this time and I knew there was a temper situation here and was waiting for it to go off. I wasn't too far off because she came up out of her chair and leaned over the desk looking directly at me. Brad stood up and moved over behind her. "I think she's a little bitch. She would cut my throat at the drop of a hat and laugh while doing it. She's a liar and would do anything to gain an advantage over someone.

"As for you, I think you're too stupid to see her for what she is a lying, back stabbing bitch that needs to die. You and your so-called command will go the same way the other aliens have gone and this time I'll be standing there cheering. I don't need you and I'll do anything I can to screw you."

She stopped dead and sat down looking at the floor between her legs. She had caught herself but too late. Her face had gone pale and her whole body was shaking. I watched her as her whole body seemed to wilt. Finally, she looked up at me and started to shake her

311

head. "My father was one of you and he left me before I was born. I have tried to find a father but none of this world will be my father. All I wanted was to be like all the other kids but no one would ever let me do that. Now you come along and want to change everything I've grown up with and I just can't let you do that."

By now I was watching her eyes closely and I could see the determination building in them. This was going to be bad and I needed to defuse it now. She was starting to fumble with her purse as I got up and moved around the desk. By the time I got to her she had her hand in her purse and was bringing it back out. I could see the butt of a hand gun as she pulled her hand up and tried to swing it toward me.

My left hand went for her right hand and my right hit her square on the side of the head. Brad moved in and grabbed her left arm and brought his left arm up and hit her in the back of the head with his elbow. With two blows hitting her within seconds she went out like a light. I removed the gun from her hand and then we laid her down on the floor. I took her purse and went through it. In side I found a small grenade as well as an extra clip for the gun.

By this time Del had got to us and was looking down on Shelah. Her face had gone pale and she had both hands gripped into fists. "What's wrong with her? She knew she couldn't do anything to you, yet she still tried. Why?"

As I looked up at Del the tears were already starting to run. She didn't like Shelah and had made no bones about it. But still what had just happened scared her and she couldn't understand what was going on. I reached over and took her by the arm and moved her over to the chair Brad had been sitting in and sat her down.

I was looking into her face. "Del, this is not of your doing. Shelah had made up her mind about this before she came into the building. She had planned an attack on us and probably had support from someone with considerable power here in the city.

"This is the battle we're entering into at this time and the reason I need the half breeds on our side. It is going to get worse before it gets better. Believe me when I tell you your life as well as everyone else in this command is at stake here. Shelah was their ace in the hole and it failed and now they're going to pay for it.

"Brad, take her out and place her into detention. I'll want to talk to her after she wakes and recovers. Make sure she has nothing with her that she can use against herself."

Brad picked her up and left the office and I went around and sat down at my desk. I looked at Del. "We have two more to interview, is that right?"

She was nodding before I had finished. "Yes, there is Brady and Charles. Brady should be here by now."

"All right go out and check and make sure someone checks him out for weapons before he passes the entry point, understand?"

She stood up and then turned back to me. "Alexander, I didn't know she was going to do that. I never thought any of them would do something like that, especially when they had an opportunity to work for some real change here in our city."

"It's all right Del, I know you didn't, none of us expected this. In the future we'll know we'll need to be careful up front and deal with any possible hazard before it comes. Now go find Brady and bring him in."

Chapter Sixteen

A New Course of Action

As Brady entered my office he was talking to Del and smiling. He was clearly a self-confident individual and seemed to handle himself well. He turned his attention to me and I motioned him to the chair in front of me. I was looking over his file when he stepped up to my desk and offered his hand. I took it and invited him to sit down. Del found her place and sat down.

I finished reading over the file of Brady's noting he was twenty-nine years old and trained in engineering. I set the file down and looked at him. "Why are you here?"

It didn't faze him, he immediately responded. "A job, I need a job and this looks like a good opportunity."

"Don't you already have a job?"

He thought for a moment. "Yes, I do, but it's more like a helper than a doer. I have little or no possibility of advancement and I am fed up with the status quo."

"What do you mean by that?"

He looked at me and then gathered himself. "Look I have talked to Del and Homer about what you're doing here. I know you are alien to this planet and the history of this city has not been too good on anyone from outside this society. I also know there are plans afoot to strike at you and your people from ambush in the not-too-distant future.

"I am a half breed which means that one of my parents was alien at the time my mother became pregnant and the linage I was born to started. I never got to know my actual father because it was just about the time that I was born when the leaders of the city started their resistance strategy. My father went with his people and died up in the caves during the fighting. I know they are planning the same thing for you and I want to stop it."

"By 'stop' what do you mean?"

He knew I was digging at him and trying to find a weak spot where his real feelings would show through. "A few minutes ago, I saw them escort Shelah out of this office. I know Shelah and she's a problem. She hates her half breed status and has tried all her adult life to overcome it. As a result, she hates anyone who is half breed and would do anything to make points by reporting on our activities.

"There are a number of those like Shelah who think if they help the leaders of the city, they will gain full citizenship, but they're wrong. This society is full of lies, deceit and greed and those in power will never share any of it with a half breed. Shelah will learn in time, but right now she is a danger to us all.

"It is my hope she was not released at this time. If she was then I can assure you the leaders of the city will know what is going on here within an hour after she leaves."

I sat there watching him and there wasn't the slightest indication that he was faking or feeding me a line. Every move and every comment were measured and to the

317

point. "What can you give to me that will assist in our overcoming this city?"

He smiled and leaned forward. "I can give you the city. You know the public powers within this city but you don't know the real hidden powers and those I know. I know where the money is and where the manpower to attack you with is at. I know how they intend to do it and where they intend to start.

"That little show you had yesterday was nothing. It was a testing and feeling out, but the real attack will come from a direction you could never expect. I know their attack plan."

"How do you know that?"

"For me it's easy because I am a tutor for the children of one of the wealthiest men in the city. His power base is deep, wide and spreading. Through him and others like him they will hit you and you will eventually have to withdraw from the city. At that time, they will then pursue and your end will be as the others." His face was hard at this time and serious. He knew what he was talking about.

I looked over at Del and she nodded. "All right Brady I think I can use you. Please go with Del and she will set up the details and your assignments starting tomorrow."

He got up and reached out to shake my hand and then turned and walked over to Del. Del came around him and advised that Charles was there and waiting. I told her to bring him in.

Del and Brady left the office and about three minutes later Del came back in with an older gentleman following. "Alexander this is Charles. Also, this is your last interview at this time."

I motioned for Charles to sit and as he did, he reached out to shake my hand. I settled back and watched him adjust himself in the chair and then he looked up and realized the chair was sitting angled to one side. He stood up and straightened it out and then sat back down. It didn't seem to bother him as he then looked at me and nodded his head.

I set the file down. "Charles you are the sixth person I have interviewed today. Four of the prior five have turned out well and one went down the tube. Unfortunately, that puts you in a position where I can pursue all the weaknesses, I have seen in those prior five people. How does that make you feel?"

He sat there and rolled his head back looking at the ceiling. He then looked back at me. "I've been here before and it doesn't bother me. I know who the prior five were and I can tell you how they did and what you can expect from them. As for me, well I feel I'm your most valuable resource for the tasks you are facing over the coming weeks.

"Please understand I don't belittle the other, except for Shelah, and I know they would do a good job for you, but I also know I am more experienced and have a greater insight into the problems you're facing and will be dealing with.

"The next issue is one of trust. In this society that is a foreign word. There is no trust here, the name of the game is every-man-for-himself and it's a dog-eat-dog environment. Trust, truth, fairness, faith, commitment, dedication and loyalty do not exist here. This is a hell of a place to live in and those who cannot work it will die.

"For the most part the other four, excluding Shelah, understand this and have survived it for all their lives. If it is your plan to change the social makeup of this city then those four and I will be of service to you. We are more than committed to seeing an end to the foundation this society functions on. It's not going to be easy, but I think it can be done."

This man knew his business and he had a good read on me as well. "Then you know we are from another dimension and our home planet was Earth, the same Earth you live on here in this dimension?"

A glint of shock shot across his face as I said that. He had to regain his composure and then answered. "No, I did not know that. You are of Earth, but from a different dimension?"

"That's right, but our Earth is nowhere near the situation you live under here on this Earth. We have not gone through the social upheaval you have gone through. We still have moral standards and ethical standards that we live by."

He sat there a few seconds thinking about what I had said so far. "An Earth with moral and ethical standards, that's an interesting state of affairs."

Now was the time to bring up my real target and purpose. "Charles it is my goal to reinstate moral and ethical standards back into this society. I know just how difficult this goal is, but I also know if I ever achieve a safe environment for my people it will have to be an environment that is conducive to our survival. Right now, this place is not.

"Once I'm finished here, I plan on moving on the next city and the next and so on until I have overcome the entirety of this world. Do you understand?" I was now leaning across the desk.

I noted he swallowed hard and then started to nod his head. "Yeah, I know what you're saying and I also agree it's going to be a hell of a job, but I think you're going at it in the right way by getting our assistance, that is with the half breeds. I warn you though, watch out for Shelah, I don't think she'll go along with it."

I had noted three people had cautioned me about Shelah; Del, Brady and Charles. It was a signal that told me to pursue their thoughts about her. "What do you mean about Shelah?"

Charles was looking me straight in the eyes. "She'll kill us all if she gets the chance."

Now it was my turn to be surprised. "Please explain?"

"She is a hateful person. She blames everyone for her being a half breed and refuses to associate with any of us. We have learned the hard way never to talk in front of her. Whatever she hears goes directly to her master and if more is needed or the actual individual needs to be identified then she will lead them directly to the person she reported on. A lot of people have died because of her. Frankly, I'm surprised she was offered the opportunity to have an interview." He was leaning back in his chair and watching me.

I looked over at Del and she was squirming in her chair. Her eyes made contact with me and she raised her hands and shrugged her shoulders. I returned my attention back to Charles. "Can you tell me what the general population of this city feels about our being here and the reaction of the powers to be?"

He smiled. "Generally, the average citizen thinks nothing of the power games going on in the running of the city. No matter who's in control their lives are what they are. They are almost as much a victim as the half breeds are, just that our law clearly places a protection over them from undue governmental interference in their lives, nothing that applies to the half breed though.

"Actually, they would love to see the current system come to an end. Their only problem is what they would be trading the current system for. I guess it's a case of the better of two evils."

That was an eye opener. I had not expected his reply, I was of the opinion the public at large accepted their current governmental system as the right way to go. I had not considered the people may be conditioned and not clearly supportive of what was over them. "You mean to tell me the people do not support the system of government they currently live under?"

Charles moved around in his seat and then reached out and placed his hands on the desk top. "I mean to tell you if you go about this right, you can get the people on your side and make the project you're working on much more likely to succeed.

"If you target the powers behind the government and take the precautions to avoid involving the general public you will succeed and the public will support you. Understand, much of the wealth, the controlling powers have is through their ability to tax the people for just about everything they need to survive.

"Let me ask you this. On your Earth did you have organizations that were considered organized criminal systems?"

324

I looked at him and started to nod my head. "Yes, we did. They were all over the world and formed up in gangs and developed armies of their own. It took a worldwide military action to finally bring them to bay."

He was nodding his head as well. "Good, then you know what I mean when I say that organized crime now runs the governments of the Earth. That is why we have city states all across this world and each one is run by its own criminal organization who uses the hard work of the people to fill their pockets with tax monies they levy on everyone."

Now I had the information I needed and it was more than I could have expected. I looked over at Del and motioned her to come over to my desk. "Del I want you to take Charles here and do the paper work on him. I then want Dominic, Homer, Victoria, Brady, and Charles in my office tomorrow at nine hundred hours. Is that clear?"

"Yes Alexander, I understand and will have them here at that time. Is there anything else?"

I had stood up and walked around to the front of my desk by this time. "Yes, there is, I want a listing of everyone involved in the government of this city as well and I want Shelah in the waiting room under armed guard at that time." I stopped and then turned to Brad. "Brad you handle the Shelah thing. Have her there at say nine forty-five hours and make sure she remains in one place and says nothing."

Both Brad and Del nodded and they headed for the door. Charles got up and followed Del and I returned to the window of my office and looked out. I had a lot of planning to do in the next few hours. I knew now what I was dealing with and I also knew I would have to become aggressive and unyielding in my dealings with these people.

Organized crime knew only one thing and that was power. Only it was a power that was brutal and direct. I would need to hit them hard and leave no one alive. Every one of them would have to go and I meant to start with Shelah. Unfortunately, she was fully aligned with these people and she would have to go.

Just her meeting with me gave her too much information to return to her master with. The next day would be the start of the conquest of Earth and a new beginning for the people of Earth and Shelah would be the key to it all.

This whole thing made my mind shift back to my home Earth and the history of organized crime in the world. It was a system that pulled criminal elements of the same race or nationality together and these formed into what we called gangs.

These gangs fought constantly trying to gain greater areas of control and the elimination of other competing gangs. The one thing that stood out was the ruthlessness they carried out their actions against one another and that would have to be my mode of operation, ruthless and without mercy.

I knew I had the tactical advantage and the weaponry advantage over the power leaders of this city. What I needed was the final identification of those power leaders and where they could be found. That was my need and it was the thing my half breed personnel would provide for me.

Looking out the window I felt there was still something else, something I was missing. It was there right in front of me and I knew it, but for the life of me I couldn't reach out and grab it. I knew this much, everything on this Earth was tied together in some way or fashion. I just had to figure that out, but my time to do so was also running out.

Shelah would be my access to the first of these power leaders. I intended to let her go, knowing full well she would be going directly to her master and reporting on what had happened. That would be my first target and it would be the signal to the others as to what they were facing so it had to be hard, over powering and ruthless. Everyone would die including Shelah.

Next, I would hunt the others down and bring an end to them. Once the current power base was eliminated, I could then institute the new governmental system and rebuilding the social structure of this city. When I was done every individual tied to these power people, in any way, would be eliminated. Not a single person who was a part of the current power of control would survive.

Yes, I had a plan and I felt I had a good plan but still something was digging at me and it was right there in front of me. It had presented itself several times while I interviewed the half breeds, but I was missing it. I needed to figure it out because it could be the one thing that makes or breaks this game.

It was right there and I knew it. What had each of the interviews brought out that touched me? It was subtle but had made itself known in each and every interview. Damn it was there and I was not finding it.

I stood there looking out the window and it was almost like a shadow moved across my field of vision and then it hit me. The ages of the half breeds ran the whole range of ages and they all referred to their alien fathers and native mothers. They all referred to their alien fathers? How the hell could they do that when those aliens were killed off around three hundred years ago?

No way, that was impossible. It was the time element, there was a problem with the time element and it was important. None of them could have met or been fathered by the aliens. Then why did they refer to their alien fathers? I felt the shock move across my face as it was setting in. The time element was all screwed up and these people did not realize it.

I grabbed the phone and dialed Brad. When he came on line I almost yelled. "Brad, get your ass down here to my office on the double and bring your gun. Now Brad now." I hung up and headed for my office door and opened it just as Brad came running up to the door.

"What the hell's going on boss?"

I walked past him and headed for the front door. "Come with me Brad and keep your eyes open. I'll explain everything to you shortly."

We left the main building and I walked across the street to the city hall and in the front door. I then walked past the reception desk and down the hall to the mayor's office and through the door. He was sitting at his desk and looked up with a shocked look of surprise on his face. "Captain what are you doing here?"

I walked around his desk pulling my .45 as I did and grabbed him by the throat. Brad stayed right behind me all the way. As I pulled the mayor up to my face and shoved the gun into the gut I said. "You have thirty seconds to tell me what the time was when the aliens were here in your city? How long had they been here? And who they mated with while here?"

The man could hardly respond and then finally got the answers out to me. As he related each answer, I grew more and more angry with the whole damn situation we were in. When he finished, I dropped him in the chair, turned and walked back to the door. At the door I stopped and turned and looked right at him. In thirty minutes, some of my people will be here and you will have a complete file laid out showing the time frame when the other aliens were here and the dates and times of each conflict between them and this city and the birth dates of each child born to them? Understand?"

He nodded his head. "Yes sir."

"If that file is not ready, I will kill you and everyone in this office. If I find one error in the file I will come back and kill you and everyone in this office. If you object in any way I will have you killed and everyone in this office. Understand?"

By now the mayor was out of his chair and almost on his knees. "I'll have everything ready at that time and it will be accurate to the letter."

I left the mayor's office and we returned to my office. Brad walked over and sat down in the chair and just looked at me. "What the hell was that all about? Shit man you just went crazy over there and if they mess up, you're committed to killing everyone in the building. Do you understand that?"

I moved around to my chair and sat down. "You damn well better believe I understand. In thirty minutes, I want you and a team to go to that place and get those files. If they are not done then start killing them and don't stop until someone comes up with that file. Understand?"

The key to what I was feeling was in that office across the street and I needed it before we started to work with the half breeds in the morning. There was something terribly wrong and I needed to find it and determine its impact on our plans and ultimate success.

It was forty-five minutes later when Brad walked in carrying a file folder and a broad smile on his face. "You should have been there. The place was in a total panic as we walked in. The mayor literally ran up to me with the file and handed to me and then dropped to his knees while I looked the file over.

"Now I understand what you were all bothered about and I think you're going to find this file most interesting." He placed the file down on my desk and then turned to me. "I'll leave the file here for you and then give you some privacy. I can see you have a lot to think about and hopefully this will give you the answers you are looking for." He then left the office.

I walked over and sat down, picked up the file and started to read.

Chapter Seventeen

The Final Battle Starts

It had been a long night. Brad had returned to my office and we had worked up the overall operational plans for the coming campaign. In a few minutes the half breed team would come in and we would start to fill in the holes in our intelligence files. Once it was done then we would deal with Shelah and her overlord.

I planned on implementing the operational plan that afternoon and hitting the power bases head on and taking them out to the person. We would then move into the population and run the remnants of the gangs down, eliminating them. The plan was scheduled for three weeks and then the reeducation of the citizens of the city and rebuilding of the social order of this city. Once this was done, we would set our sights on the next city and so on.

That morning Del came in the office and announced the five half breeds were there and ready to work. I nodded to her and asked that she take them to the conference room next door to my office. Brad and I picked up our paper work and entered the conference room from my office and I went to the seat in the middle of the table.

I turned to Del. "Is Shelah in the waiting room under guard?"

She turned to me and nodded her head. "Yes. She seems a little subdued right now, but still was hostile toward me and the guards."

That's just what I wanted to hear. I turned to the others and nodded to Brad and he walked up to the writing board. "All right the first thing we are going to address is the names and identification of the power leaders of this city. I need their names, where they live, if they have family and if the family is at that location with them, the number of soldiers in each gang and where their main hang outs were."

I watched their reactions to my request and there was little if any observable reaction. They immediately started to layout the names and locations and as they passed the pages to Brad, he entered them on the board. The information grew faster than I had anticipated and in no time, we had a listing of sixth-seven names and locations.

We then started to rearrange the listing based on the most powerful to the least. Then we added the soldier's numbers and the hang outs and any other details that were relevant to the needs for our planning. I was more than pleased with the results of the team.

It took us two hours to finish the collections and identification process. It took Brad another twenty minutes to complete the hierarchy layout of the gangs and then we sat there and started to review and make corrections to the layout. By noon it was all done. I had a complete layout of the power base for the city, the people we would be targeting in our takeover of the governing of the city and the elimination of any threat to my command.

"Good work and now I want any fringe people. Those people who hang out with the gangs but are not a gang member sometime referred to as associates."

Again, we had a listing in just minutes and that gave us the people we would need to bring in and clear on a one-on-one basis to ensure their position and attitudes toward us. This would be critical to the overall plan and would require the best judgment of the half breed team and my investigators, but I felt certain we could do it.

That was it, we had all we needed to move on the powers of this city and we formed up our strike teams. Shelah was then brought into my office under armed guard and I sat her down in front of my desk.

She was as defiant now as she had been yesterday. I sat there looking at her knowing full well I was sending her to her death, but there was no other way. If our plan was to work, she had to go and through her we would destroy the power base of this city and initiate the changes we were planning.

As I sat down across from her, she started to say something and I raised my hand to quiet her. I settled back in my chair, picked up her file. "Shelah, yesterday you as much as said you would do anything to stop me. Frankly I doubt if there is anything you could or would do to compromise our position and future here. As a result, I am going to release you and tell you if I ever see you again, I'll kill you outright. There will be no warning, no second chance. If we should run across each other in any way, shape or form I will pull my .45 and shoot you on the spot. Do you understand?"

I sat there waiting for her to respond. She was looking right at me and I could see the level of hate building in her. I had to admire her though because she did not take the bait and held herself in check. She then nodded her head yes.

I looked over at Brad and nodded my head toward her and Brad moved over and took her by the arm and lifted her out of the chair. He escorted her to the front entrance of the headquarters and sent her on her way. She never looked back but walked straight across the street and turned up the next street and was gone. Brad then turned back and walked into the building leaving Shelah to the surveillance teams.

In less than twenty minutes she entered the residence of one of the most wealthy and powerful men of the city. As it turned out he was on the top of the half breeds listing of power criminals. The stage was now set and we could begin the roundup. I looked over at Brad and nodded my head and he gave the order to carry out the attacks. In the next two hours the upper power class of the city would be in custody and ready for the ultimate in power plays this city had ever seen.

Each strike team was prepared for total war as they moved in on their assigned targets. Any sign of resistance was to be met with total annihilation including the building they were resisting from. The actions of the teams may have sounded like overkill, but I had noted on the first day, when I hung the leader of the military force who opposed me, the people of the city approved of the hanging. My feeling was that the general population lived a life of terror and fear and anytime one of these power criminals was taken down they approved.

Reports started coming in as we waited at the command center. So far, all the actions were moving ahead without any problems yet. I knew it could change at any time and was anticipating it. I hoped the shock of the hits would blunt any reactions or resistance during the arrests. My hopes were short lived.

Seven of the assigned targets had already gone down when we received word a strike team had been ambushed. An ambush, meant someone knew we were coming and the only way that could be done was by having some information passed on to them. I looked around at the half breeds looking for any signs or reactions that indicated one of them was our problem.

As the information came in the team leader did a remarkable job. They had two down wounded and then targeted in on the source of the ambush and cut loose on them. The fight raged for another ten minutes as they worked their way through the enemy. Meanwhile we had backup teams moving in from the other direction and they were successful in getting the enemy pinned between them and then they really went to work on them. Ten minutes later they had the enemy forces down and dead.

I called the team leaders. "Can you tell who they were working for?"

There was a pause and then the leader came on. "Yeah, we just found the information you wanted and it was our target power criminal."

"Is that confirmed?"

"Yes sir."

"Are you able to continue on your target?"

"Yes sir. The backup team will stay with us and we are going after that SOB now. How do you want him?"

I sat there looking around at the others, "Dead."

The team leader came back. "As you wish and with our pleasure."

The other two teams completed their missions and were returning with their prisoners. I sent two of the teams who had already returned out to provide added support to the team that had just dealt with the ambush. We hit the power criminal with an overpowering attack taking out the building and killing better than half those hold up with him.

Two hours later the rest of the team returned to the base with their target in tow. I had already determined this person would be the first one I would deal with and it would be harsh. What was to follow would be a show for the whole of the population of the city. I expected to see a heavy turnout and popular support for what we were about to do in dealing with these power criminals.

However, there was one issue that needed to be tended to and that was to determine who gave the one target a heads up in regards to our actions that were coming at him. I motioned Brad over to me and asked everyone currently in the command center remain there until we were done with our private meeting. The half breeds were advised and a guard set at the door and we, Brad and I, returned to my office for a sit down.

Once in the office I walked around my desk and sat down as Brad took the seat across from me. I could see he knew full well what we were there for. "Brad, I think you know what this is all about. Someone gave a heads up to that criminal before our strike teams headed out. Right now, I feel if anyone did, it had to be one of the half breeds. My problem is which one and how do we determine who and prove it."

He was nodding his head. "I agree, but I have no idea just who it could have been. We had the tracking teams on those people from the moment they left your office after the interview till they returned this morning.

None of them deviated from their normal activities and no phone calls were made to anyone of question at the time. I just don't know how any of them could have passed that information along."

"That, my friend, is exactly the same boat I'm sitting in. We took all the precautions we could think of and there is nothing we can point to that would incriminate any of them. Right now, I'm at a loss as to how the word got out."

We sat there again trying to think of anything we missed. Brad then asked. "Alex could it be the ambush was simply an accidental occurrence at the time we sent the strike teams out. I mean, the route they took is a common one our teams use all the time. We've already had one attempt that was actually a measuring of our alertness, but this one was not the same, this was an ambush on a street we use all the time. Could it be just a coincident?"

He had a point there. The enemy had shown they were going to fight us and had made the first move so I knew it was just a matter of time and the real push would start. That could have been just that and nothing

343

more. It then came to me. "Brad did anyone think of tracking Del during this time?"

He smiled at me. "Yeah, we did and she did nothing that indicated a problem. As far as I can tell she is clean as well."

That was good news to me. I hated even the thought I would have to deal with something like that, but I knew it was possible. "Good, at least that makes me feel better. Then you think maybe this was just a coincident and not an actual leak?"

He was still thinking about it. "Yeah, Alex I think we need to treat it that way for the time being. I would not set it aside or forget it, but right now it appears to be just that. One thing I do know, once we finish with these criminals, we should be clear of any such problems, hopefully."

I was in agreement with him and then stood up and headed for the door. "Come on we need to get back to the command center and debrief our half breeds and the team leaders."

We had successfully carried out a sweep of the city and pulled in the biggest players of the power criminal element. We now had a lot of work to do in dealing with these beings and it was not going to be pleasant. I needed a lot of input from our half breeds and what they told us would clearly determine our next step.

As we entered the command center everyone was seated at the main table except Del. She was standing over by a window with her arms crossed over her chest looking out and across the plaza. She turned when I walked in and then motioned me over to the window. As I walked up to her, she nodded her head toward the window.

"I've been watching those two men over there for ten minutes now and they seem to be involved in something concerning this building. They have split up twice and walked in opposite directions and then returned and would converse about something. I've never seen them before and they just do not seem to fit in there."

I watched the men for several minutes and then turned and motioned Brad over to the window. "Brad I want those two men over there by the water fountain brought in now."

Brad turned and left the room and several minutes later he and three other troops left the front entrance and walked across the street. As they approached the two men they split and started to walk away. Brad drew down on them and they were pushed up against the building wall. Brad was looking around and then pointed and grabbed one of the men and swung him around and ducked down behind him. The other three troops hit the deck and pulled the other man down with them.

Just then a transporter came by with several men in it and they opened up on Brad and the troops who had already started to fire. The shots of the ambushers were high and Brad's team's shots were on target. About that time rounds started coming in from behind them from the area of the front entrance to our building. The ambushers were neutralized in seconds. Any still alive were dealt with right then. Brad brought the other two into the building and to a holding room.

Brad returned to the conference room and found a chair and sat down. "They didn't belong there all right. Damn that was close. Oh, by the way there were no injuries on our side."

I walked over to him and placed my hand on his shoulder and then turned to Del. "Good work Del, now you and the others start coming up with other groups we may need to deal with tomorrow. Come on Brad, we have some interviews to carry out."

I left the command center and went to the first holding room. As I entered the man looked up at me and sat back in the chair and folded his harms across his chest. I sat down opposite him and pulled my .45 out and laid it on the table in front of me. His eyes settled on the gun and then moved up to my eyes. I hoped to hell he could read eyes really well because mine had a lot to tell him.

I sat there looking at him and then leaned forward. "I'm giving you one chance and only one chance to save your life. You're going to tell me who you work for and where they are or else, I'm going to cut you in half with that .45. You're not going to get a second chance and I'm not going to ask you a second time. Now talk."

His face had gone pale and he was having a hard time sitting still. His eyes had gone from mine to the .45 and were riveted on that gun. He knew he was on the edge and he had no place to go except to jail or dead on the floor. Finally, he raised his hands. "All right, I don't need this. I had no choice. My boss ordered me on the mission and if I refused, I was a dead man. Mark, the other guy and I were to lure someone out of your building and then the transporter team was going to gun them down. It was meant as a warning to pull back or you'll all die."

I sat there waiting and not saying a thing. Brad moved over behind the man and stood there. He could feel Brad behind him but still maintained a fixed stare on the gun. My boss is the head of the South Street Gang. His name is Stalker and he's tough as nails. He sees a chance to take control of the city with you arresting all the power people. That left a void and he's planning on filling it."

I sat there watching him. "Where is his headquarters located? I want a complete layout of the place and the number of people he has there. Got me?"

He nodded his head and started in. "He's holed up in the old Grace House Restaurant located down on the south side on Tideland Street. They fortified the place front and back. He has around forty-five people there and all are well armed."

Brad was watching him closely as he told him of the fortifications, "Anything else?"

"Yeah, he has snipers located across the street and in several building on both sides of the street approaching his place."

"What kind of weapons do the snipers have?"

He sat there looking at me. "Old military type bolt action rifles with iron sights."

"Are there any high explosives or rocket type weapons on the premises?"

"Yeah, they have five or six shoulder mounted rockets and a bunch of grenades."

Brad was sure he was being honest but, in this world, you never knew, "Anything else?"

"No, you going to kill me now?"

I was watching him; he was a man defeated and ready to die. I looked at Brad. "No, we're not going to kill you. But you will be placed in a cell and held until we decide what to do with you."

I got up and Brad walked over to the man and patted him on the shoulder and we then left the room.

I turned to the next room and opened the door and walked in. The other man was sitting there with his hands clasp together and stuck between his legs. He looked up when I entered the room and then watched as Brad walked in. He was fixated on Brad. He probably knew that Brad was one of the men they had helped target. I sat down across from him and pulled out my .45 and laid it on the table in front of me. I then leaned forward. "I'm only going to ask you once what you were up to and who were you working for. You fail to answer I'll cut you in half right where you're sitting and then throw what's left of you out in the street for the world to see."

He swallowed hard and looked at me and then the gun. He brought his right hand up and ran it through his hair and then reached out and grasped the edge of the table. "I had to. I had no choice. I had to do as I was told or die. Crap I was going to be dead one way or the other and if I did as I was told, my family would probably be left alone.

"Man, I didn't have a choice in this thing and now I'm a dead man. I wasn't armed and had no intention of shooting anyone. I was the bait and that was all. You know what happens to the bait don't you? It dies every time."

This guy was even more scared than the first one. I watched him for several minutes as his insides crawled. "Who were you there for?"

"Stalker, he pulled us in off the street and told us what we were to do and if we didn't, they could kill our families to the last person."

"You're not one of his gang?"

"No sir. I'm just me and I have a family I work for and care for. I have never been involved in anything illegal or violent. I didn't want to be here, but I had to. He would have killed everything I treasure.

I sat back and nodded my head and then stood up. "We'll be keeping you here for a little longer, understand?"

He nodded his head. "Yes sir."

I then left the room and headed back to the command center. As I entered the room, I noted the wall board covered with names. At the top was Stalker. I walked over to the board and took the pen and circled that name. I then turned to Brad. "Kill him."

Everyone in the place started looking around at each other. I then stepped to the head of the table and laid out what had happened. "Three hours ago, a bait and kill game was initiated against this facility. Thanks to Del we were on top of it before it could fully develop. The game goes like this. A gang leader finds one, two or three people and forces them to carry out a series of suspicious actions near one of our posts.

"When we see these people or action, our people are sent to investigate what is going on and while involved in that activity the gang comes in at high speed and opens up on the troops and the bait people. They failed this time and we got the name of the gang leader who initiated the game.

"Now it's our turn and we are going to kill him and his entire gang, family, and friends. Everyone goes down to the last person. When the next gang does it, we do the same thing. It won't take long before they tie the two events together and these games come to a stop, any questions?"

There were none. Meanwhile strike teams were entering all the buildings on the block of the gang's headquarters. Their targets were the sniper posts that were said to be in many of the buildings around the restaurant. Within ten minutes the first sniper was located and neutralized. In the next hour every building had been swept through and cleared of any threats.

Next the assault unit deployed at the rear of the restaurant and the assault started. They had set up for a frontal attack and failed to adequately cover the rear. We went through them like they were warm butter. In the end we killed sixty-nine gang members and took Stalker prisoner. He was returned to our facility and placed in a holding room. Brad and I went to talk to him.

As I entered the room, I was met with a barrage of words most of us prefer not to hear at any given time. I moved over to the table and sat down opposite him and waited. He continued to scream and insult me for the next ten minutes until he finally ran out of anything to say that was new. I then pulled my .45 and laid it across my chest with my right hand holding the grip and my finger on the trigger.

That got his attention and he settled back in the chair and sat there looking at me. "Now that you're done being a horse's ass, maybe we can talk. You seem to think you're some kind of king pin around these parts, don't you?"

He sat there looking at my gun and then moved his eyes up to mine. They were hard eyes, killer's eyes, but they were scared eyes as well. "What the hell you think you're doing tearing my restaurant apart and killing my people like that?"

"I'm cleaning out a rat's nest, that's what."

He took two deep breaths. "How would you like me to take that gun of your and shove it up your ass?"

I smiled. "Come and get it."

He sat there looking at my eyes and I'm sure he was seeing me begging him to try, just try. He shifted his eyes to Brad and then back to me. It was clear he was measuring his position and likelihood of being successful in any attempt to take me out. As he sat there considering his situation, I was shaking my head and still smiling at him. "Where do we go from here?"

I stood up and holstered my gun. "Son, you are going to help me bring these war games to an end. In about two hours you and your survivors will walk out into that street and in front of the whole city you will be hung by the neck. I'm more than a little sure the last thing you will hear will be the applause from the citizens as you are hanged."

I turned and walked to the door and looked back at him. "When I'm finished there won't be a single person like you left in this city. It will be the first time these people have breathed a breath of air that did not stink with your presence. Good luck in hell."

He sat there looking at me. He started to say something and then looked down at the floor and started to cry. It was the same with all these big guys, once they're caught and cannot throw large numbers of people at you, they break down and beg. Well, it's too late and its payback time for all they have done to the people of this city.

Brad and I closed and locked the door and headed back to the command center. The new team was still there finishing up their listings of power criminals and gang leaders. As I watched them finishing up, I called them all back to the table and sat down with them. I had a new idea and I wanted to bounce it off them.

Once they were all seated and ready to hear my idea I started. "Over the past few days, I have noticed one thing missing from this city and its a newspaper."

Almost immediately everyone sat up and started looking around. I had definitely hit on something. So, I continued. "Now, I am proposing you, as a team, start to publish a newspaper but I have a special need for this paper and it's the truth. I want you to publish the truth about anything and everything. That includes my command and our purpose here. There is going to be a storm of truth coming out of this paper and I will accept nothing short of that."

I was watching them and they were all beginning to smile. In short order that changed to a grin and then all hell broke loose. They started talking between themselves and almost forgot I was there. Finally, they stopped and looked over at me. I was sitting there waiting knowing full well I had started something that couldn't be stopped. Finally, Del asked. "Alex, are you serious about a newspaper?"

I was nodding my head. "Absolutely I am. The people of this city must start to receive the truth and they must learn what the truth is and what it looks like. If we want to make changes here, we are going to have to lead the way and not just point the way."

She sat there looking at me. "That means we can address anything we want and put it before the people?"

I think maybe I just created something I may wish I hadn't. "I mean you will present to the city a clear and concise record of everything that is going on in the city. No one is immune to being in the news and that goes for me and my command as well. Naturally I expect all stories and a preview copy to pass over my desk before it goes in to full publishing. My purpose will not be to censor, but to ensure the truth is in fact being presented.

"I want you to organize this paper and to determine who will be the senior editor and who fills which positions. I expect a completed layout of your organization and a policy statement in three days' time. Once we have completed and approved that, you can then start picking and writing stories.

"Right now, I want a weekly up and running in about two weeks and we'll determine whether it needs to go daily later on. Are there any questions?"

There were none and I stood up and thanked them and headed for my office. Brad was walking beside me and shaking his head. "Boy do you know how to stir things up. Do you know what's going to happen when they publish their first paper?"

"No Brad I don't, but I'm hoping it will stir the pot and get the people of this city to start thinking about their current situation and there is a better system out there if their willing to work for it.

"I think what will come out of this group will be something we will profit from in every conceivable way. Anyway, we'll see. Tomorrow I want to get the executions over with. I think the people are waiting for it and they need it as well. Anyway, one way or the other, things are about to change big-time around here."

Chapter Eighteen

Nothing Goes the Way It Should

This was going to be one of the most important days for my command over the people of this city. As I sat there at the breakfast table my mind was running over all that had happened over these few months, from the battle with the plants to the realization this place, this planet we were on was actually Earth.

The scope of that revelation had hit me hard and then to learn we were actually on the North American continent and where the United States had once been had been the final kicker. Damn this has been one strange situation overall.

I was watching the troops and civilian staff walking into the mess hall and trying to determine if there was any actual difference in their overall appearance. That's an odd thing to be thinking about right now, but it crossed my mind if this was Earth, even though it was in another dimension, then there should be little differences in their physical makeup. Yet there was something there, something I couldn't put my finger on, but it was there.

Just then Brad walked up and sat down across from me. He sat there looking at me, "You all right?"

At first, I didn't hear him and then he reached over and touched my hand and repeated his question. "Alex, are you, all right?"

I looked right at him and then realized he had asked me a question that jolted me awake. "Right, yeah I'm all right. I was just thinking and observing everyone as they came in the mess hall."

We sat there. "And, what were you observing?"

I raised my hand for a second acknowledging I heard him and I would answer shortly and then watched as Del and one of her half-breed friends came through the door. I looked at Brad. "Brad, I've been sitting here watching everyone come into the hall and it came to me there were no actual differences between our troops and the people of this city. As I mulled that over in my mind, I started to see things I had not seen before. Nothing big actually, but things that were clearly different, know what I mean?"

Brad turned and looked over at the line and then around the hall trying to grasp what I was talking about. "Alex, I really don't see any difference in these people from us except for their dress. What are you talking about?"

I focused back on Brad and then looked down at my hands and then back to Brad. "Brad, there are differences and I'm not sure if I'm just seeing things or have actually started to really see what is here. At first, I thought it was physical but now I'm certain that is not the issue, it's under the surface, it's mental and it could kill us."

The file I had gotten from the mayor's office started to bring everything together and I didn't like what I was seeing. Now it was becoming clear and now I needed to act on it and act fast. I knew then and there we were in a death trap and we needed to act fast.

By now I had his attention and he was beginning to get it, Alex you're scaring me, look on his face. He was trying to say something when I waved him quiet. "Don't say anything but hear me out. There is something here we have missed and I think I know what it is. I can tell you here and now we're in deep trouble and it's just about ready to land on us."

I stood up and leaned over toward him. "Get the troops formed up and in full battle gear, do it now."

He jumped up and headed out as I headed for the door. Just then Del came up to me and I grabbed her arm and walked her out the door and to my office. I sat her down in the chair and leaned over her. "All right young lady, it's time you tell me everything that is going on here and don't leave anything out. You know what I'm talking about and you have thirty seconds to talk to me or I'm going to kill you and every breed in this city."

She had a shocked look flash across her face and then she stood. I shoved her back down into the seat and then put my face right into hers. "Del I know what is going on, but I need you to talk to me. No more playing around. Your life and that of everyone else at this base are on the line, so talk to me."

She slumped in the chair and then looked back up at me. "We were just trying to get out of here, to get to safety. We've been tolerated all our lives and we felt you were the way out. I didn't mean any harm to you we just wanted to get out and away from here."

I moved back and around to my chair and sat down. Just then Brad came through the door. He looked at Del and then to me. "Troops are forming up in full battle gear now. Alex what the hell is going on here?"

I looked at Brad and then at Del. "All right Brad, I want the entire command and the breed civilian working with us to move out of the city and back across the wall and up on the ridge. Set up a battle line and prepare for a total engagement. Do it now Brad and no questions asked?"

Brad saluted and turned and headed out the door. I got up and walked around and grabbed Del and headed for the door as well. When I got outside the command was formed and moving out. I signaled Brad that I wanted double time and the troops responded. In less than half an hour we were outside the city gates and moving fast.

I pulled up and detailed a plasma gun to setup to cover our rear. I then set two teams to our left and right to cover for actions on those two fronts. Twenty minutes later we were at the wall and the entire command moved over the wall and up the ridge. We had caught the city flat footed and they could not respond fast enough to stop us.

Once on the ridge we set up a strong defense and then waited. It was then I took Brad and my other command officers aside and had them sit down. I then had Del stand before them. "All right Del, now's the time to tell us everything. No more playing the game, you must tell us and tell us now."

She stood there looking at us and then took a deep breath. "We were just trying to get out of there. We have lived under them for all these years and this was our one chance to get away. We are breeds, but we are a special breed, that is we are all human. The aliens from the past came to this place and tried to become part of our society. They married with the women and then started having children. What they didn't know was that some of the children were human and some of them were not.

"When they finally discovered that it was too late and they were killed to the last man. We, the breeds, were left and the city decided to let us live because we were of their kind, though not their species."

She stopped and let that sink in and then looked at me. "You fought for your lives on the other side of the mountains against the plants. When you came over here on this side you thought you had found beings like you. But you didn't, you see they are all plants."

There it was and the file had filled everything else in. This was unreal, but I knew we were on the verge of total disaster. The file had referred to others within their social order as slaves. I had heard nothing about slaves before but things were starting to generate an idea. Del and her friends were breeds and there was another resident of the city and they were slaves. The only thing I could think of was that the slaves came from other wars where captives had been taken. It then touched me that they were human as well.

I sat there looking at her and then realized everyone was watching me. My head was full of questions but I couldn't think just how to start asking them. She was scared half to death and knew she was in real trouble. I finally centered on Del. "Del that means you are part plant?"

She shook her head. "No, it doesn't work that way. When one of you mates with a citizen one or the other becomes dominant and the resulting child will be 100% human or plant. Those of us who were 100% human have been tolerated and we live as you have found us."

"Are there any human societies anywhere on this planet?"

She nodded her head. "Yes, there are. I understand the bulk of them are to the west of here, how far I don't know."

"What about the giants?"

"They too were plant, just a different variety. They were a natural enemy of the plants in the city and behind the wall and they have battled for as long as history goes back."

"Del, what can we expect next?"

She looked out at the wall. "They have been cultivating an army ever since you arrived and destroyed the current army. The crop is almost fully developed and would have been ready in another two weeks. You have that long to move out or get ready."

"How big an army is it that you're talking about?"

"It will be in the millions."

I stood up and turned to Brad. "All right get the troops moving. We're going back to the caves and then heading west. We have two weeks to get this mess straightened out and then we had better be long gone."

It took us two days to get back to the caves and then I ordered the factory to produce as many transporters as they could in a week. Make them large and fast. We then set to work increasing our communications and armament so we could lay down a line of fire that could handle the size army coming after us.

Finally, I had a chance to address the breeds. I still was not sure as to whether they were human or plant life and so I had the medics pull them all together and start to conduct physicals to make the human vs. plant determination. As it turned out all were human and we had that problem off our backs but it opened up another one.

There was no indication of any plant presence in their bodies. That meant they were the creation of a mating between two humans and not a human and a plant. That

367

question is where did they come from? There were only two possibilities, one, there were women with the aliens who landed here and these people were the children of those alien couples. The other was that the aliens had had relationships with human slaves the plants had taken captive sometime in the past.

However, there was one other possibility and that was these people were not part alien but were in fact the offspring of slave mothers and fathers. Those were the choices and there could be no other.

Now it fit, now I knew. The aliens had been here around three hundred years ago and if they had any children they would have been with slaves and not plants. The breeds we had with us were a combination of alien and slave humans and there was no other possibility.

Del had stated they were the product of a mating between a female plant and a male human. Our medics advised that DNA analysis showed there was no plant elements involved. They had to be one of the three possibilities. Bottom line they were human through and through and we would treat them as such.

I then took Del into the office and sat her down. I had a question I needed to ask and she needed to answer and do it now. "Del, you have been with us for two months now and during that time you said nothing to us about the people actually being plants and not human, why?"

She sat there looking at me. I knew she had to answer and I gave her all the time she needed to respond. Finally, she sat up and looked at me. "Alex, you would have never believed me if I had told you. Yes, I knew they were plant life and I did not tell you, but if I had you would not have believed what I told you and I would have died the moment I left your building. Whether you believe me or not, I intended to inform you once you actually started the executions. At the time they would not have been able to get at me and we would have been in control.

"I blew it because I failed to understand the level, they would go to in order to destroy you. I discovered they were going to fight back with everything they had and once I found out I knew they would be growing an army. The fact is all the breeds knew this was coming, but we were in a no man's land and were not totally under your protection at that time.

"Once we got past that point, we, I, have not held anything back from you. Our lives are on the line too and we don't want to fall captive to them again. If we do, they have a special treatment for us as they kill us. We would become a garden for their new leader clan that they must regrow now. Instead of planting their seeds in the earth they would plant them in us and the seeds would sprout and they would eat us from the inside out."

Crap, what a hell of a place and life this is. I then looked at her. "Del I'll accept that reasoning from you. It does not change the fact I think you were playing it too close for the rest of us, but I can also see the situation you were in. That is now behind us.

"There is one other thing you and the others need to know. That is, you are not half-breeds you are 100% human. This can only mean you came from one of three possibilities. Either the aliens who were both male and female or you resulted from a coupling between aliens and human slaves being held by the plants or the only other possibility is your parents were both human slaves. Do you understand? What I need now is to have you and the other breeds take the lead and get us to hell out of here. Can you do that?"

She sat up her mouth was wide open as she took in the fact, she was not a breed but probably a slave child. She then stood and walked around my desk to me and took my hand and placed it on her heart. "We're 100% human? That changes everything from here out. Alex, I swear to you here and now I will die before I will let you down again. We, the other breeds and I will lead you to the human populations to the west. We have never been there, but we know the route well because we have studied it while planning our own escape from here in the past.

"One thing you need to do and be ready for when we leave, and that is the ability to set the forest and grass lands on fire. That will work as a barrier for us and they will burn for weeks. If there is one thing, they fear above all else it is fire and especially forest fires."

That I had not thought of. I called Brad in and laid everything out for him and then ordered him to set up the means of setting their world on fire as we moved out of this area to the west. He smiled. "That is one job I will enjoy immensely. We'll put together a system that will burn the memory of us into their minds for the rest of their existence, however short that may be."

He started to leave and then stopped at the door and slowly turned and looked right at me. A smile worked its way across his face. "Boss, what would you think if we booby trapped some fires. I could set up napalm bombs that work on a proximity fuse with a timer. That way an army could follow us and the leading edge of the army could pass over and charge the bombs. We could give them a ten-minute delay and then when they went off not only would they start a forest fire but they would prime that forest fire with an army fire."

When Brad becomes devious, he is the best. I looked at him and then to Del, she was smiling, then back to Brad. "Yeah, that is genius and something I should have thought of. Do it and plan on spreading them all over the landscape as we move west."

We had two weeks to pack and get moving and put some distance between us and the coming army. Having worked round the clock we managed to produce enough transporters to carry our entire command with several extra for equipment and replacements if any broke down. We did that all in a week.

On the morning of the first day of the second week we were ready to move out. We placed the base on self-defense and closed it down.

I sent four scout units out ahead to both sides and to our rear. With the rear scout unit went the booby trap units who would set up our little surprises for the coming army. I figured we could cover easily three hundred miles a day and if necessary four hundred. I took the lead and Brad took the rear area and we headed out.

I figured we had seven to ten days head start on the plant army and that would put us at two thousand to three thousand miles out before they moved on us. Del thought we only had to go around a thousand five hundred miles to get to the human region of the continent. That would be five days so I thought we were way ahead of the plants and let myself become over confident. The fact was we would be barely a day ahead of them.

The first sign they were on us came the next morning. We were up and moving when Brad came on line to me. "Alex the booby traps are going off behind us. We made a quick run back on our tracks and spotted them coming. The traps are decimating them but their numbers are unbelievable. I would estimate there were easily two and a half to three million of them coming. They're on foot, we have the speed to out run them and keep going, but I don't think we'll be able to stop or rest any until we're to our destination."

"All right Brad, we'll up our speed and you start spreading those bombs as thick as you can. Set them for a thirty second delay and set them in wave formation. Got that?"

He responded to the affirmative and we then upped our speed. I called Del up to my position. As she rode up beside me, I looked over at her and then advised what we had just learned.

A look of confusion crossed her face and she then yelled. "They've been growing that army since day one. We need to watch our sides they may have set up some ambushes for us out here. I never saw any of the new army and that tells me they were sent out early and are ahead of us."

I looked over at her and then yelled. "They sent a blocking force ahead of us and they plan on having us in a box and then cutting us to pieces. I have a little surprise for them."

I then called Brad. "Brad?"

Brad came over to me, "Yeah Alex."

"Brad, they have a blocking force ahead of us probably near the border with the humans. We need to put plan Alpha into effect now. Total involvement, understand?"

"Understand Alex, total involvement."

Del was looking at me with an expression of total confusion. "You planned on this didn't you?"

I smiled back at her. "Yes, my dear we did. One thing we learned over on the other side of the mountain is no matter their numbers when faced with a plow plants are helpless."

"Plow? What the hell are you talking about Alex?"

"Del, our plasma guns can cut the earth to a depth of ten to twelve feet and it literally plows the earth in to a froth of dirt and anything else in it. Now that we know what they're up to we can set up for them and show them what a farmer can really do. In the next two hours you will see the full impact of our plasma guns and the plants will learn a lesson and realize what is to come once I make it to the human lands."

As we approached the region felt to be the most conducive to an ambush the transporters with the plasma guns mounted on them moved into position. Our scout unit had finally located the enemy and determined the extent and formation of their forces. They had set themselves up in an arch across our path of travel. Once in range they would cut us down like grass.

The rear guard advised the following army was in the midst of a huge fire storm and they would be tied up for some time. We could now concentrate on the enemy in front of us. Once we hit a point a half mile from the enemy lines, we fired up the plasma guns. At first, we simply flattened the ground in front of us out and then as we came in on them, we drove the plasma beams into the earth and started the process.

We hit their line with full force literally tearing them apart. They were throwing everything they had at us and making scores when the second bank of plasma gun came on line over the next quarter mile the ground before us was completely churned up and laid bare. Their guns finally went silent as we finished off the remainder of their troops and then stopped. I brought the plasma guns around facing the opposite direction and then we reversed our course.

Those following us never expected to see us coming at them. We hit them with every plasma gun going at high output. What was left of their army after the fires was literally minced and ground into the earth. We made sure there were no survivors. Once done we again reversed and headed for the human region.

As we drove through the ambush site there was quietness, not even the wind was blowing. We passed on through and by evening crossed over and into the human region. Our next task was to locate and make contact with any human representatives and see if we were on friendly lands.

We needed a bivouac location and then we needed to see to our wounded and killed, if any.

Chapter Nineteen

Human Meets Human

There was an obvious change in the terrain as we left the lands of the plants and entered the human domain. Not knowing anything about those who lived here I decided to make ourselves vulnerable to those who may be watching. We found an open area and formed up our command into a defensive position and set up our bivouac. We posted guards and set the automated scanners in operation. All was set and we were ready to wait and see what happened next.

Nothing happened that night and by early morning I was thinking about moving on when I got this feeling we needed to stay put. I sent scout units out in the direction we came from to ensure we had no visitors from the plant army we left behind. It was just about mid-morning when the first signs of others took place.

Off in the distance, on a small hill we observed a lone individual on what appeared to be a horse. He was there maybe five minutes and then rode off away from us and behind the hill. The entire camp was brought on alert and we set up waiting for what was to come next. We didn't have long.

It was twenty to thirty minutes later when they came in force. I would estimate the count at around two thousand five hundred men on horse and on foot. They came in on us in a single file formation and circled our encampment, staying about a hundred yards out from us. They continued to circle us until our entire encampment was encircled and then stopped and faced inward toward us and held their position.

Brad walked up to me. "What do you think?"

I looked at him and then back out toward our visitors. "That was an impressive approach they made. They're disciplined and well trained. They're not going to throw themselves at us like the plants did. No, they're going to measure us out and then make an approach. After that it's any one's guess."

"Do you think it may be better if we tried to make the first approach?"

I was busy watching and locating the leader of this unit. I had finally located him and was looking right at him, as was he looking at me. The way he sat his horse and looked around the area told me this was a strong and well experienced being. He was not a fool and he would not throw his command away unless it was necessary.

No, he was one I could deal with and wanted to meet one on one. "Brad, we'll sit and wait. They're not going to do anything dumb. No, their checking us out just as I am checking them out. We'll wait and let them make the first contact attempt."

It was now a waiting game and I had no idea just how long it would go. I only knew the next move was his and I would wait until that time. I turned and walked to my tent and entered and walked over to my desk and sat down. When I did the rest of my command went about their normal daily activities, but ready to take the lines at a second's notice, I was prepared to sit there and wait for as long as it took.

As night came upon us, we spotted camp fires flaring up around our encampment. We did the same, life as usual and no surprises. We settled down for the night with no unusual events during the night. The next morning, I exited my tent to see the entire unit of the visitors again on their horses and sitting as they did the day before. It was noon when their line broke and opened up and a contingency of people moved through the opening heading toward our encampment.

The commander of the unit was one of those coming toward us. In total there were ten of them all well-built and clearly experienced in what they were doing. As they approached, I walked over to the edge of our lines and stood there watching them. When they were within fifty yards they stopped and the unit commander dismounted his horse and stood there looking at me. I raised my right hand and he did the same in response.

He then started walking toward me and I in turn started toward him. As we approached each other we came to a stop at a comfortable distance from one another. He was looking me over and then offered his hand, something I had not expected and I responded in kind. As we gripped one another hands he spoke. "Do you speak as we do?"

His grip was firm but not challenging as was mine. "Yes, I do."

He looked over my shoulder. "What kind of weapon is that you used against the Weeds yesterday?"

The name he used for the plants almost made me laugh, but I restrained myself and answered. "Those are plasma guns."

"Do you plan on using them against us?"

Now we were getting down to business. "Not unless we have to. We are here in peace and do not wish to use any weapons against anyone unless we are forced to."

He was nodding his head and then his head leaned to his left as he looked down at my belt and the .45 holstered there. "That is your weapon?"

I looked down at it and then back to him. "Yes, this is my weapon."

He was watching me intently now. "That's a Colt 1911 .45 automatic. They are rare and anyone carrying one is a great warrior."

That stunned me and I almost forget to answer him. "Yes, it is a special weapon and one I would die for before giving it up.

He then dropped his hand. "You will not die here. You are welcome and we invite you to our council meeting this evening if you desire to come."

Now I had to take a chance. We were two strong warriors standing face to face and if it is like any other place in all of creation, warriors of our caliber were honest and honored our words. "I will be there and be honored to come to your council meeting."

With that he nodded and turned and walked to his horse and mounted and rode off. I walked back to the line and went to my tent to prepare for the coming meeting. Del fell in behind me as did Brad and we all three entered the tent. "What was that all about?"

"Brad, I've been invited to their council meeting tonight."

There was a pause, "You going?"

I turned to the two of them and looked Brad in the eyes. "Yes, I'm going. This is the time to take the chance and trust these people have honor and want peace. Besides I have no choice, I must go."

Del then stepped up to me. "Alexander this is not a smart thing to do. You are placing too much trust in them and that is not smart."

I looked at both of them. They were concerned and for that I was grateful, but I needed to go. "Listen you two, that warrior leader will never let anything happen to me at their council meeting. He would die before that would happen. This is a man of honor and when he looked at my .45, I knew full well we were brothers as well. No, I will go and it will be me alone."

The time had come and I walked out of the camp area and stood there waiting for what came next. A short time later a single horseman came out of the line with a second horse in tow. The horseman rode up to me, stopped and turned the horse he was leading to me. I step around the horse and mounted nodding to the horseman I was ready to go. It had been a long time since I had been on a horse, but it felt good. So, there I was in full uniform and riding off with an alien human to a meeting with hopefully the leaders of these humans and possibly the start of a new life.

As we passed through their lines they pulled back and made a wide opening for me to pass through. There was no noise or signs that would indicate a problem. If anything, it was a sign of respect. As we cleared the ridge, I saw a large tent ahead of me surrounded by a large contingent of troops. We stopped at the entrance to the tent and as I dismounted my friend from the prior meeting walked out to meet me. He offered me his hand and I took it. "My name is Jahoshaphat I am the leader of the Clear River Clan. I welcome you."

I felt a strong tie between myself and this being. "My name is Alexander and I am the commanding officer of the Star Field Force Unit 943rd. I thank you for your hospitality."

With his left hand he showed me the way to the meeting. As I entered the tent there were at least thirty others present. All stood up as Jahoshaphat and I entered the tent and moved to the head of the table. Jahoshaphat offered me a seat and I bowed my head and sat down as he sat beside me. Once seated, he clapped his hands and a door opened at the side of the tent and a number of people entered carrying an assortment of foods all of which looked wonderful.

He turned his attention back to me. "Where do you come from?"

385

There was no getting around it I had to be honest with this being and lay it all out for him. I decided to work in to the alien thing slowly. "We are from the plant region of this place. Our story is involved and maybe a little hard to believe but if you're willing to hear me out then I will tell you everything?"

He nodded his head. "I am interested, please continue."

So, I told him everything that had happened to me and my command right up to when they found us here at this time. All during this time he sat there eating and listening intently to everything I said. When I finished, he then turned to me. "So, you are not of this planet and actually come from a different dimension?"

I nodded my head in agreement and then gave him more detail as to how our coming here to this place happened. I found myself rather surprised by the fact he seemed to understand what I was saying and I was in fact alien to this planet. What really seemed to touch him was the issue with our coming from another dimension. How this would play out I was not sure, but I had his attention anyway.

We had finished the meal and the others were sitting back and relaxing as

Jahoshaphat and I continued to talk. It was now his turn to tell me who he was and where they had come from. "Alexander, we are a tribe of people who have lived in this place for many generations. The history of this planet is not a nice one and it is one we are working hard to recover from. During the Great War many nuclear weapons had been used and that resulted in strange things happening to the life forms of this planet. As you have learned one of those was the creation of intelligent plant life.

"The area you have come out of was particularly hard hit with many nuclear weapons. At one time a great nation stood here in this place. Its governing central location was in the east in the area you have come out of. As a result, huge genetic changes took place in all life forms there. In time the plants became the dominant controlling life form. Those of us in the west did not suffer as severe a reaction because fewer nuclear weapons landed here. There have been some genetic issues, but for the most part nothing of major concern.

"When you entered our region, you were about half way across this continent. That line was set many decades ago and has held steady ever since. In this half of the continent there are about thirty tribes all living in and controlling specific areas of this western half. Yes, we have had wars and from time to time still do, but for the most part we are at peace and have learned to stand together against any encroachment by the plants. I guess you would say my region is on the front lines in holding the line against the plants. They are always trying and testing our resolve and we continue to resist.

"We have witnessed your actions against that plant army and wish to learn more from you and how you did what you did the other day. We have never seen a plant army so completely destroyed by a much smaller force. Your weaponry is most extraordinary and we are most interested in. It is our desire to form a relationship with you and your clan and work together building a better resistance against the plants. Is that a problem for you?"

There it was, the reason for his approach and attitude toward our presence. We were two warrior leaders and one had impressed the other and now there was an offer to form a partnership. We would become a part of this clan. I looked him in the eyes. "Jahoshaphat you are a great warrior and leader; I can see that. I am an alien to this planet of yours and I seek a place where we can live, and live-in relative peace. We did not ask to come here, but fate put us here and now we must make the best of it.

"I want to accept your offer, but I have a problem. You see I want to go back to the east and remove the plants from all that territory. I need an army big enough so we may move across the whole of the land and wipe all intelligent plant life out of it. No compromise and no negotiations, they must all go. That is what I am after and that is what I am proposing to you.

"Come with me, and you and any other clan that wishes to join us, will spread across the land and bring the glory of the old nation back to life. I have a strong feeling the east coast of this land is open and free for the taking. The plants are not there because they fear the residual effects of the nuclear war. What they don't know is time has removed the effects left by the war and as a result all that is there is open for the taking.

"From there I think we can move across the rest of the world and bring the old Earth back to its past glory. What say you?"

He sat there looking at me. His mind was spinning with thought and ideas. "You feel we could actually do that?"

"Not only can we do it, but we will do it. All I need is an army of well trained and disciplined men and we can take this continent and then the world. There is nothing we can't do. All we must do is form up and join together for a common cause. Again, I ask, what say you?"

He sat there looking at me and then his eyes went down to my .45. I followed them as they looked at my gun. It was a treasure, but I knew it would buy me an army. I stood up and removed the holster and gun and laid them down on the table in front of him. "As a gesture of good faith, I give you this gun and ask that you wear it well."

He looked at the weapon and then me and then back to the weapon. It was a heavy situation and he was making the decision that would make or break my plans. This was no stupid man. He had dreams and goals and all he needed was the cause and I brought that to him. He slowly reached over and placed his left hand on the gun and then offered his right hand to me. "I offer my allegiance to you. We will follow you wherever you choose and I am sure I can get most of the other clans to join in. We have dreamed of this day and now it is upon us. For that we will celebrate."

The word went out and the lines around my command were dropped and Jahoshaphat rode with me back to my base and we entered and laid out what had happened. Brad walked up to me and put his hand on my shoulders. "Today we start to fulfill your dreams."

That was twenty years ago. The human army was formed and we started out across the lands of the plants bringing total and complete destruction to them. Our first goal was the caves and once there we built the weapons an army of this size would need. It took us a year to build everything we needed and to train the forces in the use of the weapons and transporters.

During this time, we had gone back to the city and completely wiped it out down to the last being. On that day we met Shelah again. She had made her choice and stood strong with the plant side and died with them then and there. Those were the testing days, the time we spent building a method and means for moving into a plant area and clearing it of any intelligent plant presence.

We learned to identify and find plant reproduction fields and to sterilize those fields so nothing could be produced out of them. It was time to move on and take the rest of the continent for ourselves but there was one other small project I wanted to address.

A large contingency of our line troops moved through the caves and onto the mountain side overlooking the valley we had originally landed in. My purpose here was to completely clear this land of any and all plant life. Nothing would be left behind. It was stripped bare and left that way never to produce another life form of any kind.

Chapter Twenty

The Building of a Nation

There it was the eastern ocean and the entirety of the continent had been taken from the plants. I had no idea what was out there waiting for us on the other side, but I knew we had the power and means of moving on. The whole of the world was before us and we would have it all before we stopped.

During this time Del and I became more than just employee and employer. She eventually submitted to me as my wife and we had produced five children two girls and three boys. My original troops had assimilated into the other clans and were now a complete part of this world.

The whole of the land behind us had been moved into and settled by different clans all with allegiance to me. The old nation that had been here was again growing and becoming a vital part of the world scene.

While searching through what was left of the great cities on the east coast, we found references to the names of the cities and this nation as a whole. It had been called the United States of America and had consisted of fifty plus states all spread across this land and out into the western and eastern oceans. We determined we would bring her back to her old glory and then let the rest of the world know we were once again.

I have no idea as to whatever happened to the old Star Field Fleet and right now that was unimportant. It was old history and this place; this new Earth was my place now and would be until my death.

Death, that was an odd concept in that humans did not die here. That is, they did not die from old age or disease. Yes, they died from battle or accidents or whatever, but old age, no.

Whatever the Great War did it created an atmosphere that brought about longevity in the human race, at least in this part of the world. Right now, I have no idea how long one may live but I have learned there are those among us who are going on three hundred years of age. That will give me all the time I need to address the rest of the Earth.

They have changed my title as well. I am now known as the Great, Alexander the Great that is. I don't know how great I am, but if that's what they wish to know me as then who am I to argue anyway. One must fulfill the position one is placed in and mine was to lead this new world to its past glory and beyond.

The breeds who came with us twenty years ago had done their research and determined there were old nations to the north and to the south of us and we shifted our planning to address those nations first. I knew that on this new Earth of ours those nations would be known as Canada and Mexico. By using the old maps, we found in a place call DC, Washington D.C., we determined the western hemisphere still existed. Our plans shifted to the conquest of the western land mass first and then we would address the rest of the world.

Almost daily my people were finding and discovering new things and ideas that had long been dead. We had located what we learned were large libraries that had an endless supply of books and computer records we could go into and use. It took us three years to get the electrical issues worked out and on line and once we did, we were bringing back to life technologies long dormant and in need of considerable repair.

Fate had placed my military unit in this place never to be able to return to our native world. What we found was more than we could have ever imagined in our wildest dreams. Now the world was mine and the human race was on the rebound. With care and a firm belief in the honor of morale and ethical standards we would bring this world back to it old glory and have the peace we all longed for.